THE LAST GUNDOWN

A town without mercy, a land without heart or soul: that was what bounty hunter Shell Dunbar confronted during that endless blazing summer. Even the handful of men who supported him gave him no chance of surviving that murderous summer of hate. They had already given him up for dead when he faced the last gundown . . .

MATT JAMES

THE LAST GUNDOWN

Complete and Unabridged

LINFORD
Leicester

First published in Great Britain in 2010 by
Robert Hale Limited
London

First Linford Edition
published 2011
by arrangement with
Robert Hale Limited
London

British Library CIP Data

James, Matt.
   The last gundown. - -
   (Linford western library)
   1. Western stories.
   2. Large type books.
   I. Title II. Series
   823.9'2–dc22

   ISBN 978–1–4448–0878–0

Published by
F. A. Thorpe (Publishing)
Anstey, Leicestershire

Set by Words & Graphics Ltd.
Anstey, Leicestershire
Printed and bound in Great Britain by
T. J. International Ltd., Padstow, Cornwall

This book is printed on acid-free paper

1

All Aboard the Flyer

Shacklock glared at the brass ball of the westering sun. Would it never set?

Hipping round in the saddle, the outlaw saw them coming still, closer now than they'd been all that harrowing afternoon. Should the possemen gain a further hundred yards they would draw within rifle range.

He kicked his horse cruelly. The animal lifted its labouring gait for several strides, then fell back into its shuffling walk-trot again. It was beaten.

Shacklock ran his eyes over his partners' mounts. Tom Lee's round-bellied calico looked to be in even worse shape than his own gelding. But Joe Ralls's stallion was moving easily enough, way out in front.

Shacklock fingered the walnut butt of

his six-gun and his expression turned hard. Could be he might just have to shoot old Joe out from under that stiff-brimmed black hat of his and commandeer his stallion before this caper was over . . .

A nervous twitch ran down Shacklock's left arm as he forgot his wound for the moment and made to scratch his beard. Pain grabbed him. The killer swore feelingly and straightened the arm to stare at the crusted blood. It hurt like hell but he still figured he'd been lucky. Who'd have ever reckoned that bunch of milksop towners would have found the guts to gang up on them as they'd done anyway? It would be a long cold day in hell before he would forget their hair-raising run out from Mesa with seemingly every gun in that lousy town thundering bullets around their ears.

Tom Lee moved his horse up closer, a big-nosed badman, angular of shoulder and hip.

'My hoss ain't goin' to make it much

farther, Gil. How about yours?'

Shacklock spat into the drifting red dust of the Rawson Plains. 'It'll get me there all right.'

'Where?'

'Where do you figure? Wagoner's Switch, of course.'

Tom Lee blinked. 'You mean we're still gonna try for a train?'

'Not try. We're gonna do it.'

Haggard-eyed, Tom Lee stared westward where that sluggish sun was sliding down towards the jagged spine of the Sundance Hills with agonizing slowness.

The hills appeared no closer than they had an hour ago, or the hour before that.

Their plan, after sticking up the the Texas National Bank in Mesa, using played-out horses, had been to make their easy way across the plains to the Sundances, pick up the Southbound at daybreak and travel south in comfort for the Pecos. But that was before many things went wrong, before Naylor got gunned down by a gutsy bank teller and before twenty angry townsmen had taken guns to them.

For a man who'd killed so often and so carelessly, ugly Tom Lee had a passionate regard for human life — when it came to his own. This concern showed plainly in his sweat-streaked face and red-rimmed eyes as he turned appealingly to Shacklock.

'Gil, we just ain't gonna make it that far. And even if we did, that train ain't due till sunup. They'd have had time to take us six times by then. We're goin' to have to change our plans, is all.'

'We already got one, pard. We're catchin' the Katy Flyer at midnight instead.'

'There's a midnight train?'

Detecting the disbelief in the other's voice, Shacklock sneered through his coarse crop of ginger beard stubble. Even after a year together on the owlhoot, Lee still didn't give him full credit for his talent of planning ahead. When plotting this run out, Shacklock had made sure he memorized all the running times for trains in the region over a period of several days, just in the event something should go wrong.

But of course Lee and Ralls wouldn't expect him to do that.

Those two never saw further ahead than the next bottle or the next woman. Naylor had been the only one with any brains. And now he was gone, downed in a thunderclap of Colts in a no-account Texas town. It was true what they said; the pick of the crop was always taken first.

'There's a midnight train and we're goin' to be aboard her, pard,' he said with an air of finality. 'Now shut your trap and save your breath on account you're bound to need all the wind you got before this night's out.'

Anything but comforted, but effectively silenced, Tom Lee moved ahead a horse length and from there on concentrated solely on getting the last ounce of pace from his plodding calico's weary legs. Shacklock took to touching up his gelding with the lighted tip of his cigar, while up front Joe Ralls's stallion continued to hold its steady pace.

The hot afternoon died hard.

The possemen drew within rifle range just on sunset and from then until dark the outlaws had a hard time of it, twisting through the foothills with inaccurate lead pinging about them. They'd not been pressed this hard since the bounty hunter, Dunbar, had come within an ace of putting an end to their bloody careers at Fort Portales a week earlier and the harassed Shacklock found himself thanking whatever god watched over the fortunes of bank robbers and killers that the Mesa posse didn't have a genuine marksman of the bounty hunter's calibre in their ranks.

Darkness was never more welcome.

Drawing rein on a broken-back ridge somewhere in the Sundance foothills, the outlaws stepped down and moved away from their hard-blowing horses to listen intently. No sound of hoofbeats. The possemen would have been forced to halt until moonrise. But if the moon should be as bright as it had been the previous night, they should have little difficulty in picking up their sign now. And the worst aspect was, one of the horses had gone lame. It was finished.

Shacklock looked south. He calculated they had about an hour's lead by this.

'Hey, where you goin', Gil?' Ralls called in sharp alarm as the leader lighted a stogie and strode west.

'Reconnoitrin',' came the terse reply and Shacklock was gone, swallowed up by the trees, leaving three winded horses and two shaky hardcases to await the rising of the Texas moon.

The speed of Shacklock's stride would have surprised his pursuers had they witnessed his long-legged progress through the mountain shadows. They might figure that with a bullet in the arm plus half a day's chase behind him he should be about on his last legs by this. Ralls and Lee were both close to exhaustion. But not him. He could always dig into himself and find a well of unused energy whenever he needed it, and he surely needed it tonight.

His strong sense of direction told him that Wagoner's Switch station lay west, north-west from the hills, and he calculated that the railroad lay some ten miles distant beyond the switchback range. The outlaw was confident he could make that distance by midnight on foot if it came to the worst. But not with possemen breathing down his neck.

So the possemen would have to be either halted or wiped out. Sounded simple when you said it quick.

A shimmering glow off to the south heralded the arrival of the moon some time later as he stood staring along a narrow-walled gorge which angled sharply some distance ahead.

He was thoughtful. He'd hoped for a better defensive position than this, but the situation here was that one of them would have to stay behind and delay the pursuit at the gorge while the other two high-tailed.

He rejoined his pards and made the situation plain, letting it sink in as he produced three sticks. 'Short stick gets to play hero, boys,' he announced with that dangerous smile of his. 'One man could hold this ravine against them possemen indefinitely,' he told two suddenly pale segundoes. 'So, let's get it decided.'

It was no good objecting, no point in reminding Gil Shacklock that his sleight of hand with cards and dice was notorious in havens where bad men gathered to relax and plan their villainy. To have done so would have been to risk arousing the Shacklock wrath, and Ralls and Lee would sooner take their chances against the possemen than do that.

Ralls drew the short straw.

Shacklock's big hand dropped on the suddenly ashen badman's shoulder.

'Pard,' he said movingly, 'I've seen it all in my time, but I'm proud to say I never rode the river with a better man than you, and the day I forget the name of brave Joe Ralls is the day I hope my breath turns sour and chokes me to death. You're a brave man for takin' a bad break so well. So long, old pard. *Adios.*'

It was the first genuine compliment Joe Ralls had ever received from his leader. Dazed by it, the outlaw somehow actually managed to raise a grin and wished them luck as the two swung up to gallop off into the darkness. But that brief glow of bravado only lasted until the first of the possemen came loping into range and just as he realized that Shacklock had switched horses on him.

'You're a double-dealin' dirty snake bastard, Shacklock!' he said emotionally, and jerked up his rifle as trouble came at him fast.

'Double-dealin' son of a bitch!' Ralls roared as he lined up his sights. But by this it was far too late.

Thundering through the rough hills, Shacklock and Lee heard the snarling crash of gunfire fade away to a stutter, a murmur and then it was gone.

Shacklock thumped his barrel chest and cried emotionally, 'A genuine hero — and one hundred per cent proof, by God!'

Tom Lee said nothing. He was silently thanking his Maker that he was a one hundred per cent survivor — astride the best horse.

It was just after eleven by Shacklock's fat turnip watch when they raised the tracks. They gleamed silver and welcoming under the moonlight below them, twisting down from the north-east from Mesa and curving gracefully on southwards to the tiny trackside building that comprised, in its entirety, Wagoner's Switch.

A sleepy depot clerk sold them tickets to the Pecos River and if the man was alarmed by their wild, beat-up appearance and the guns, he gave no sign. He affirmed between yawns that the Katy Flyer was running on time, was due in at midnight.

Resting aching bodies on the battered

old depot bench, the outlaws sat smoking with their ears cocked for one of two sounds; the beat of hoofs or the murmuring clatter of the train. Neither spoke until they glimpsed the tiny finger of light to the north-west, and this was Shacklock's signal to get emotional again.

'That Ralls,' he declared, shaking his shaggy head. 'He stood 'em off, pard. I tell you, when we get to the Pecos, you and me are goin' to have to erect some kind of monument to that brave boy.'

Taciturn Lee just nodded. He knew full well there wouldn't be any monument. Come tomorrow, if he was to mention the name 'Joe Ralls', Shacklock's reaction would most likely be, 'Joe who?'. It was a tough life on the owlhoot and only the very hardest survived it.

And it was only then, with the loco headlight in clear view now, that big-nosed Tom Lee fully realized they were going to survive after all.

Ever since the bounty hunter Dunbar

had picked up their scent in the Cedar Breaks three weeks earlier, Lee had lived with the presentiment of his coming doom. Maybe it was the knowledge that it was Dunbar who was coming after him — surely one of the most feared names on the outlaw trails of the West. Then again, it might have been that snaggle-toothed old gypsy fortune-teller in Clantonville who'd read his grubby palm, then refused point-blank to divulge whatever it was she had seen there.

But the last and most likely possibility was that ever-strengthening hunch he'd developed that he'd used up all his luck in the most dangerous profession in the West.

It could have been any of these factors, or even a combination of all three.

Whatever, Tom Lee now made a fervent vow that when he left the Katy Flyer at the Pecos he would say goodbye to it all forever — the outlaw trails, Shacklock, the lawdogs and that constant threatening demon named Bad Luck.

He would settle somewhere sleepy and raise chickens with that bad-tempered tart from the Bucket of Blood Saloon and cultivate a paunch, or else his name was not Thomas George Washington Lee.

The two came erect as the train rounded the last curve and came rumbling and clanking down the straight stretch towards them.

It was a short train, comprising loco, tender, one car and a caboose. The loco was squat with a high bell stack and flashy yellow woodwork. The firebox cast a crimson splash upon the tracks as the engine belched out steam and began to slow. Soft yellow lights glowed warmly fromn the single car and they saw someone toss a cigar butt from a window and it fell silently, a bouncing red eye in the shadows.

Shacklock expanded his chest as the depot agent wandered out toting a grey mail satchel. The wild man couldn't even feel his damaged arm now. He felt ten feet tall and knew with a powerful sense of certainty that there was simply no way he could lose.

He smiled cheerfully at engineer and fireman as they peered down from the loco, their faces ruddy in the fire glow. He clapped his skinny companion on the back as the lighted car slid by them and came to a halt.

'All aboard for the Pecos, old pard,' he laughed boisterously and headed for the car door with a long, muscular stride that nothing could slow.

He stopped when he saw the man standing in the doorway.

He was tall and wide-shouldered with his hat tilted over his eyes and he toted a shotgun held in the crook of his arm. He made no effort to alight as the two approached, nor did he back up to give them room to board. He simply stood there with his face in shadow, the eyes beneath the hatbrim narrowed to a steely gleam.

Shacklock stopped sharply, his owlhoot-trained senses triggering a warning to the brain. In his eagerness to clamber aboard, Tom Lee cannoned into him, almost fell, cursed, then broke off as he too realized something seemed to be wrong.

'Gil!' he breathed, eyeing the man. 'What in the Sam Hill — ?'

He broke off as Shacklock jerked up his Winchester and dropped back into a low crouch.

But the stranger's shotgun was now at firing level and the voice behind was laced with authority and menace. 'Reach or die, outlaws!'

A sound, more animal than human rasped from Shacklock's throat. Yet his alarm in no way hampered his blinding speed as his rifle swept up and was within inches of reaching firing level when the shotgun erupted.

For one hellish moment both train and depot were illuminated by a shimmering blue glow that accompanied the deep-throated roar of the shotgun. Ripped through and through by lethal pellets of lead delivered at close range, Gil Shacklock went over backwards, still clutching his unfired rifle, screaming horrifically although no ear could hear him above the shotgun's awful blast.

Swifter than he'd ever been, Tom Lee palmed his Colt as he hurled himself violently to one side, triggering as he fell. The bullet shattered a window and the clash of glass mingled with the shotgun's second thunderclap of sound.

Lee hit the platform with both knees, jaws stretched to their limit in his now silent agony. The gun fell from his fingers. He sank lower and toppled on to his side, kicked out once then died thinking of the bad-tempered girl from the Bucket of Blood Saloon.

Shacklock was still alive, sliding like some broken-backed worm, leaving a crimson smear in his wake. He was mouthing meaningless sounds and struggled to bring his gun muzzle to bear upon the tall figure stepping down from the train, now clutching a big Colt .45 in his right hand.

'Quit, Shacklock!'

He heard the voice as though it came from a great distance. He knew how bad it was, but couldn't quit. Not now, or ever. His finger jerked trigger and he had the small satisfaction of seeing the menacing figure duck beneath the shot. Then the six-gun smoked once more and he felt white hot death go through him like a jagged Apache war lance.

Dust on his lips, shadowy wingbeats in the air above him.

'Bastard!' he choked.

'The name is Dunbar!'

Dunbar! He should have known. He tried to burden his killer with a dying man's last curse but he choked on his own blood.

★　★　★

Beyond the clutter of buildings known as San Paulo the yellow desert grass sizzled upon the burning flats, and rounded hills rippled and palpitated beneath rising heat waves. Beyond lay ugly ridges pocked with outcroppings of dead-looking grey rock. In the middle distance, the bulk of the Sourdough Mountain range loomed like a grounded blue cloud on the horizon, sombre and smouldering.

San Paulo matched its bleak surrounds.

Here, the monotonous drabness of unpainted clapboard was unrelieved. Dull-eyed women moved sluggishly from one dreary store to another or else worked at washing clothing in the shade of the sparse trees by the river.

This was a place where mangy dogs and scraggy hogs rooted for sustenance in the back alleys with half-naked children playing, shrieking and fighting amongst them.

And all the time, buzzards circled lazily overhead, gliding through the vagrant dust devils which occasionally rose before the erratic push of the hot wind blowing in from the Seven Sisters Desert.

The telegraph office did nothing to improve the look of Main Street any

19

more than did the ancient telegrapher who sat at his desk studying the message he'd just received from distant Feather River.

'Dunbar,' he muttered, frowning through wire-framed spectacles. He stifled a yawn. 'We know any Dunbar?'

Telegrapher's assistant, Willard Price, scratched the back of his scrawny neck.

'Nope,' he said finally.

'You sure?'

'Ummf!' the youth grunted. It was too hot to exert his meagre mentality.

'Shell Dubar,' his superior persisted, giving his chair a good kick. 'Try harder.'

Being too old and tired to socialize any more, the old man left it to his off-sider to keep abreast of the numbers of drifters, hardcases and border riff-raff who made San Paulo an even rougher and more dangerous place to live than needs be.

'Er, could be that feller what fell in the hog waller yesterday,' was the best his junior could come up with.

'He the same geezer what fell through the eatery window recent?'

'Uh-huh. He's a regular fallin' fool.'

'*His* name's Clanton. I remember his name from when he fell off of Daisy Clinton's dray.' The telegrapher showed a faint glimmer of interest, but then shook his grizzled head. 'Nope, try again.'

'Who's that wire from? Mebbe that'll give us a clue.'

'Ranger Station at Feather River . . . ' The oldster studied the yellow slip. 'Captain Frank Dobie.'

'A Ranger? No Ranger knows nobody from San Paulo. What's it say?'

'He wants this here Dunbar pilgrim to contact him.'

Willard Price groaned with the effort of conjuring up mental images of the floating population that made its headquarters across at the Crying Shame Saloon. Ponderously he fitted faces with names, suddenly snapped his fingers.

'Got it! The big jasper!'

'What big jasper?'

'Why, the big jasper what threw Hudd Mitchell into the horse trough last night.'

'Oh, that big jasper.' The telegrapher pondered a moment. 'Don't see him the breed of jasper a Ranger captain'd know. But I guess it's worth a try. Take this across and see.'

'Can't it wait till later?'

'How much later?'

'Well, dark-down when it's cooler.'

'Take it and git!'

It was only fifty yards from jailhouse to saloon but Price was still dawdling his way across several minutes later when he sighted something that caused him to sharpen up and take notice. Immediately he straightened, finger-combed his unruly hair snapped his red braces before striding across to the young woman alighting from her buckboard.

'Mornin', Miss Amy,' he beamed.

Amy Stolbeck surveyed him gravely over her horse's hindquarters. The prettiest young woman in the county had a disconcertingly direct manner that successfully kept San Paulo's mashers at arm's length.

'You have pie crust on your chin, Willard,' she remarked, and turned away to mount the steps.

Price flushed furiously and swabbed at his face. He was angry with himself and with her, yet his annoyance faded as he watched her pause for a word with the Widow Willigan.

He unconsciously licked his lips as he noted how snugly those tight-fitting denim pants defined and shaped the girl's rear view, while the way she tossed her curls and laughed at something the widow said was enough to fill any young telegraph operator's head with the craziest notions.

But eventually the girl vanished into the cold gloom of the store, leaving him with no option but to continue on to the Crying Shame.

Out front he saw a long row of dusty ponies standing hipshot and stirring restlessly when tormented by flies.

Further along were four big horses that Price had never seen before and he noted that each animal carried a sheathed saddle rifle.

More strangers in town, he mused. And if past experiences counted for anything, he expected that the old formula of 'Town plus Strangers equals Trouble' would likely prove itself again.

He entered the cool gloom of the saloon, pausing to assimilate the atmosphere.

In sharp contrast to the town itself, the Crying Shame was almost exotic and colourful. Lounging at tables dotted about the earthpacked floor, men dozed, played cards, got drunk or started fights — whatever took their fancy. There were slit-eyed *hombres* whose faces on Wanted dodgers ornamented many a law office, as well as the telegraph office he worked from. There were swarthy Mexes with tiny conchas tinkling around the brims of outsized sombreros; cowhands, miners, gamblers and drifters and more than one citizen who could justly lay claim to having never done an honest day's work in his life.

He paused to inhale deeply. He loved this steamy atmosphere.

Squinting through the tobacco haze Price stood just inside the swinging doors searching for a face and sifting the various voices, the nasal twang of the northerners and the soft Spanish drawls of the Southerners all reaching him through the sad and poignant music of a guitar, its strings plucked by a plump woman wearing bright red gaiters.

Shell Dunbar had seen the young telegrapher come in through a whiskey haze. He stood at the far end of the long unplaned bar with a lighted cigarette dangling from one corner of his mouth and eyes half-closed against the rising smoke. His grey gaze flicked over the youth without much interest and focused upon the chubby guitar player until he realized the young man was making directly towards him.

'Mr Dunbar?' Price was respectful. It mostly paid to show respect within the Crying Shame, particularly when they came tall and broad like this one.

Dunbar didn't reply. He was staring at the yellow telegraph slip in the youngster's hand.

'Got me a wire for Mr Shell Dunbar,' the youth said.

'From Captain Dobie?' Dunbar queried. He had a big voice to go with his husky frame.

Trice grinned. 'Correct. You was expectin' it?'

Dunbar nodded slowly. He'd been expecting it right enough, even though he could never quite figure how Frank Dobie managed to keep tabs on his bounty hunters . . . even the ones with a habit of losing themselves in some hell-hole or another when a job turned bloody or bad.

'What's it say, son?'

'Don't you want to read it?'

'Sure don't.'

'Well, the captain wants that you

26

should contact him.'

'Forget it.'

'Huh?'

Dunbar fished money from his pants pocket. 'How much will it cost for you to send a return wire saying forget it?'

'Well, about thirty cents, I guess. But, mister — '

Dunbar pocketed the slip and thrust a dollar bill into the youth's hand. 'Go send it, boy, and buy yourself a new hat with the change.'

Willard flushed with pleasure; it was his first tip.

'Why, thanks a whole heap, Mr Dunbar. I'll go get it off right away,' he said and turned to go, naïvely believing he'd met the first genuine gentleman ever to set foot in down-at-heel San Paulo.

'Oh, and son — ' Dunbar called after him.

Price turned, beaming eagerly.

'Yes, sir, Mr Dunbar, sir.'

'Go wipe your face. You've got pie crust on it.'

2

The Big Fight

Shell Dunbar took another drink.

The reflection that stared moodily back at him from the fly-specked mirror behind the bar showed a broad, strong-boned face with hard lines etched at the corners of the mouth. Grey eyes, one of them still discoloured from last night's brawl with that loud-mouthed drunk. He was in bad need of a shave.

A saddletramp, was what the mirror showed.

But the mirror was wrong, for it was merely reflecting the features of a young man, not yet twenty-five, who made his living in one of the most dangerous professions in the West.

Bounty hunter.

Most times Dunbar was proud of his

calling, for he was as dedicated to justice as any man who wore a lawman's star. But at odd other times, like today, the negatives of the bounty-hunting business seemed to outweigh the pros heavily.

At such times he was prone to drink more than was good for him, to seek solitude and moodily consider the advantages of several alternative occupations, such as cowpunching or riding the wagon trains.

Pouring another, he took out the crumpled telegraph slip. Again. Captain Dobie had wired him $2,000 by return five days earlier in Mesa. Five hundred iron men for the head of Tom Lee, a full fifteen hundred for Gil Shacklock.

Alive or dead — preferably the latter.

With his wire, the captain had also requested details on how Dunbar had managed to take the outlaws after they had eluded the Mesa posse, but this he had failed to do.

He might have easily explained how he'd patiently questioned the fourth gang member, Lou Naylor, while the possemen were off shooting up the brush. Naylor had spilled Shacklock's orginal plan to catch the train at Wagoner's Switch and Dunbar had figured that the surviving trio might still head on to the depot, even though pressed hard, and there try for an earlier train.

He could have told him how he'd taken a train south and come face to face with Shacklock and Lee at the depot just as the train blew in — and blasted them out of their boots with a shotgun when they failed to surrender as ordered.

But he didn't.

With the money in his belt, all he'd been interested in was holing up and getting enough whiskey inside him to drown out the gurgling, choking sounds Gil Shacklock had made going down with a load of buckshot and a .45 slug in his guts.

Now Dobie wanted him to make contact. Another plush job lined up, no doubt. Well, they would be setting up ice cream parlours in Hades before he would hit the trail after the next bad bunch, he promised himself solemnly.

And this time he meant it, forgetting deliberately the last time he had quit the bounty-hunter trade for ever. And the time before that.

The plump girl playing the piano struck a sour note.

'Shut up that consarned racket!' bawled a rough-looking customer with a bushy black beard.

Dunbar turned to put a slow stare on the man. He was one of a party of four who'd come in together an hour before. Looked like owlhoot, the bounty man reflected moodily. They all did, come to think of it. But, reminding himself he was no longer interested in law-breakers, he took another swig and turned his back. The girl continued playing. Blackbeard slammed down his cards and kicked a chair over.

'I sure enough don't like repeatin' myself!' he announced truculently.

She played on. It took more than curses and abuse to distract a girl who made her living playing for the bums, rumdums and human garbage that frequented the good old Crying Shame.

The man with the beard grabbed a glass and heaved it across the room in the girl's direction. It missed its target, although not by much. In flight, it bounced off the skull of a hard-rock miner who erupted to his feet, cursing like a muleskinner. When he figured out who'd tossed the glass the drunk stumbled across to the table and punched Blackbeard squarely in the teeth.

The brawl that ensued was something of a classic — noisy and violent — and for many like Dunbar, enjoyable to watch. It helped take his mind off other matters to see two grown men battering one another on to the critical list with bottles, chair legs and anything that came to hand. But when Blackbeard missed his target completely with a wickedly wielded straight-back chair and the hurtling missile slammed against Dunbar's knees, he momentarily lost his temper and went charging into the fray — something he'd never have done sober.

He homed in on Blackbeard and didn't miss.

The big man went down with a crash under a brutal right hook, and Dunbar was grinning hugely before a hurled bottle of gin and bitters bounced off the back of his head and sent him to his knees.

Before he could recover, one of Blackbeard's bunch caught him across the back of the neck with a rabbit-killer and knocked him on to his face.

The blow hurt like hell. But more significantly, it half-sobered him and, where he'd merely been sore before, now he was good and mad.

Spitting Crying Shame dirt, he came erect, sleeved his mouth, identified the king-hitter and went in swinging.

Later, the saloon's clients would rate the Dunbar performance in the big brawl as one of the most spectacular ever seen in this rough corner of the county. The longer he punched faces and kicked groins the better he was feeling, until the angry sheep-herder with the patriarchal white beard came up behind him and brought a heavy teakwood plank down on the back of his skull with enough force to stun a grizzly bear.

It stunned the bounty hunter.

He knew he was down on his knees, knew he had no hope of rising either now or later, when above the racket came a shout, 'Look out, Dunbar, he's got a gun!'

It was the barkeeper's voice and the sheer panic he heard in it saw him dive wildly behind the piano abandoned by its player only moments before.

Two shots thundered and the old open-top shook under the impact of angry bullets.

He was stone-cold sober in an instant. A brawl was good fun but this was turning into something else. Rising above the piano he sighted Blackbeard holding a smoking six-gun while brave men on all sides ducked for cover.

'You-you busted my nose, goddamn you!' the man howled drunkenly, and up came that big Colt again, not fast, but not all that slow either.

Dunbar had mere seconds to come to a decision; risk his life by going on with a meaningless drunken ruckus — or run.

Running went against the grain but not half as much as did killing a man — or getting killed — over nothing much at all.

He ducked, dived and charged headlong down the sloping rear exit with the crash of shots and howls of drunken rage filling the saloon he was leaving in his dust.

Back on his feet in the cool air of the saloon's back yard, Dunbar darted to a window and glimpsed a sight which should not have surprised him, yet did. In clear view directly beneath a swinging oil lamp, with a dozen drunks urging them on, a giant timbercutter from Frog Hollow was trading angry blows with . . . Blackbeard!

Dunbar first frowned, then grinned. He shook his head eventually and chuckled as he turned away from a saloon that seemed to be rocking on its hinges, so fierce was the two-man encounter taking place beneath its bat-infested roof.

It was a long time since he'd allowed weariness, circumstances and his own aggression to get the better of him. He put this down to too long on the trail and maybe too much danger faced over recent times. But he was lucky to get out of it, he knew, as he followed the narrow alley for the main street, and was so busy reassuring himself he missed the last step, tripped up and stumbled forward on to the porch of the Fashion House Salon.

He swore, laughed and was rising when the voice reached him: 'I swear it must be true, what they say. Whoever it was who said the only difference between men and pigs is that pigs are good for eating!'

Now, Dunbar had been through a lot. He could have been killed, admitted to drinking too much in the saloon, was relieved to have escaped a wild man with a gun — and so was in anything but the right mood to find himself under attack again.

He got up fast, ready to wrangle, but halted with his jaw hanging open. No fewer than three frowning but attractive young women stood on the flower-decorated front porch of a dress shop in full skirts and bonnets, tapping their parasols on the porchboards and staring at him as if he was a tramp.

His anger fading, he looked down and realized he looked like a tramp.

'Is this the one, girls?' The handsomest of the three was indicating him with a furled parasol with lace tassels on the handle. She was plainly contemptuous, but for some reason the longer he stared at that perfect oval of a face and flashing blue eyes the less he felt insulted, beaten up or even sore. 'Is this the one who started that disgusting fight next door?'

'Guilty as charged . . . er, ma'am?' he answered for them. He put on a smile. 'Want to hear what happened so you won't think the worst of me. And by the way, my name's Dunbar, if that means anything.'

The beauty looked him up and down scornfully. 'Honestly, the more I see of the male species the more they seem to resemble hogs!' She swung away, arms full of expensive-looking packages, moving like silk on those long, lissom legs. 'With apologies to the swine, of course.'

He could scarce deny the accusation, he realized, as he stared down at himself, all covered in dust and blood. He felt disgust rise in his throat and concluded instantly that instead of hanging tough and looking to cement his niche amongst the hard men here, he might well take a good look at himself — through her eyes.

He did so and didn't like what he saw. And wondered that — if a cat could look at a queen — might not a bounty hunter somehow figure out a way to make a better impression on the most breath-taking if totally unimpressed female he'd ever seen?

He could try.

But not right away, of course.

He headed off along the street past the saloon where fights were still raging, didn't stop until he spotted the boldly lettered sign across Main Street.

It read:

BODIE BURNS, TONSORIAL
PARLOUR AND BATHHOUSE
NO ANIMALS ALLOWED

He sniffed. Something didn't smell that good.

He fitted his hat to his head and headed straight across the street. Fast.

★ ★ ★

Dunbar was spotless.

Standing before a full-length mirror an hour later in freshly pressed pants and a borrowed hickory shirt, he looked and felt a new man. He'd shaved, washed and soaked while Bodie Burns dusted, brushed and pressed his pants, boots, hat and even gunbelt. He was aware that he carried a subtle yet identifiable aroma of lavender water.

Bodie had even persuaded him to camouflage the black eye with a light dusting of talcum powder. He knew he looked close to his best and was relieved to see that the lovely dark-haired girl was still loading packages into her buckboard out front of Summerhaze's General Store.

He approached hesitantly, conscious of an unfamiliar nervousness.

She really was an uncommonly attractive woman up close with the dark and glossy hair, blue eyes and faultless figure. She would have stood out any place, and doubly so in San Paulo where the fat lady with the guitar at the

Crying Shame might be regarded as somewhat better than the local average. Added to that, he mused, there was something about her that went beyond mere appearance — a touch of mystery, perhaps?

He touched hatbrim as the girl and the storekeeper grew aware of him standing on the opposite flank of the buckboard.

'Miss,' he said, 'I'd like to apologize for what happened outside the Fashion House Saloon.'

She surveyed him gravely in a way he found disconcerting, for there was no telling what was going on behind those remarkable eyes. He darted an appealing look at the storekeeper as the silence held. He'd purchased some equipment from Lothar Summerhaze yesterday and had paid for it in cash money — something that should impress any San Paulo tradesman.

The pudgy storekeeper finally caught on, noisily cleared his throat.

'Er, this here is Shell Dunbar, Miss

41

Amy. Shell Dunbar, Miss Amy Stolbeck.'

'Introductions aren't necessary, Mr
Summerhaze,' she said coldly, turning
for the doors. 'Mr Dunbar and I have
already met.'

Shrugging apologetically, Summerhaze turned and followed her back
inside the store. When they emerged
some time later with more packages,
they found him still standing by the
buckboard.

Straightaway he offered to help with
her purchases but it was all too obvious
how she regarded this overture as she
continued packing things away, with her
back turned.

But Dunbar was nothing if not
persistent.

'Got far to travel, Miss Amy? I'd be
pleased to ride escort, for this sure isn't
any country for a young lady to be
travelling on her lonesome.'

'Nor are the main streets of this very
town,' she responded, climbing up and
settling in the high seat. 'Thank you,

Mr Summerhaze, and good day,' she added and wheeled the buckboard away to travel down the centre of the street towards the hotel.

'Just who is that little lady, storekeeper?' Dunbar asked, climbing the steps.

'Daughter of old Rooney Stolbeck, Dunbar.' Summerhaze swabbed sweat from his face with a spotted kerchief. 'Rooney's got himself some sort of a gold mine out in the Seven Sisters. Never shows in town himself. A bit tetched, if you ask me, what with his high and mighty ideas about things. Thinks he's better'n everybody else, but I'm cussed if I know why.'

Dunbar watched the buckboard roll to a halt before the hotel and the girl stepped down.

'You means she lives out in the desert with just her father?' he asked wonderingly.

'Keerect. Ain't no life for a gopher, much less a purty gal like that. Still, it don't appear to bother her none, so I guess that's the main thing.'

'Where is this mine?'

Summerhaze's gaze turned sharp. 'That I don't know, on account nobody seems to know. But even if I did know wouldn't be tellin' nobody on account gold has been known to give off a powerful scent that can attract some mighty mean rats.'

Dunbar moved off without comment, making no attempt to correct the man's obvious impression that he might well come under the heading of 'rats' himself, for all he knew.

He headed directly for Gravy Abe's Diner, not too despondent about his failure to make any impression on a girl he'd really felt he wanted to impress, concentrated instead on ordering up a good square meal and lighting up maybe the best cigarette of a busy day.

After he'd eaten he could start making plans for moving on and forgetting a girl with sky-blue eyes.

At no stage had the bounty man taken any notice of the men sprawled lazily upon the store bench. He didn't glance their way now as he stepped down from the porch. For their part, the loungers were beginning to drowse off again, now that brief distraction from flies and dust seemed to be over.

With one exception.

His name was Moe Archer and he was Blackbeard's sidekick from the Crying Shame Saloon. There was nothing drowsy or uninterested about Archer, nor had there been ever since storekeeper Summerhaze first dropped that magic world 'gold'.

As Dunbar's broad-shouldered form receded down the street, Archer rose lithely and headed back up to the saloon, causing a hound dog sprawled beneath the stage depot landing to sit up sharply and start in barking. The dog was startled. Nobody ever moved that fast on a sleepy San Paulo afternoon.

3

The Deadly Lure

'Gold!'

Black-bearded Luke Claggett rolled the word around his mouth as if it was a plug of high-grade chaw tobacco. He smacked meaty lips and nodded across the table at Archer.

'Better tell us more, Moe.'

Archer obliged and his audience of three, Claggett, Jimmy Ellington and Jack Lomas, gave him their undivided attention. They listened like men who knew what it was like to live hard, men who knew every deep-gut hunger there was, and the most powerful of these was for gold.

Behind them were stone walls, iron bars and the eternal stink of cooking cabbage and unwashed bodies. Back in Redemption Penitentiary, it had been

46

breakfast of corn bread and gravy, ten hours a day plaiting hackamores and stitching army saddles in the leather shop, with a smile in the mouth or a cut from a bullwhip if ever a convict spoke out of turn.

Back there, a man could get to feel he'd been born in that stone prison, where the only strong emotion a man ever felt was — hate.

Here, it was so very different, after all the iron bars and stone walls and grinding discipline. In sweltering San Paulo there was no law and no restrictions on a man other than those dictated by his own abilities. Here there was hot, greasy food, all the raw whiskey a man could drink, women within easy reach and the companionship of pards you'd served hard time with.

Yet even so, here in San Paulo, as had been the case in Redemption and before that on the owlhoot trails of New Mexico, the old complaint was still the same.

Empty pockets.

They'd picked up horses and a few stolen dollars on their way east from New Mexico but were desperately in need of real money. And the most real and lustrous currency of all was gold.

When Moe Archer eventually finished relating the scraps of talk he'd overheard up at the store, Luke Claggett took out a fat black stogie and set it between his teeth. Ellington was quick with a light, for big Claggett was as much the boss man here in the free world as he had been in Redemption Penitentiary, where his iron fists had made him king of the rat-heap.

It was not until he had his stogie going to his satisfaction that Claggett started to speak in his hill-billy drawl that was as Southern as sorghum, molasses and mint juleps.

Claggett declared that the idea of a girl and her old man operating some kind of gold mine out in the desert sounded promising enough, or at least far more so than anything they'd been able to latch on to in San Paulo thus far

— which tallied up to zero. After a pause he nodded his shaggy head and admitted that this just might prove to be the lucky break they so urgently needed.

Jimmy Ellington grinned hugely, then winced, forgetting the busted lip he'd taken from Dunbar in the big ruckus.

He said, 'So how do we go about it, Luke? Mebbe grab her when she quits town and make her tell us where her and her pa hang their hats?' He licked swollen lips. 'With any luck, she'll make us force it out of her.'

'Always got but the one thing on that poor, undernourished brain of yours, ain't you, Jimmy?' remarked Archer. 'This here is business, boy, and business and funnin' just don't mix nohow.'

'Reckon we all know what Jimmy's got in mind, Luke,' said Lomas. 'But ain't his idea still the best we got?'

Claggett blew a perfect smoke ring. The leader's mood was serious. He'd caught the whiff of real money in Archer's story of the gold mine and he wasn't about to stand by and see themselves louse up the deal as they'd done so many times since quitting the Big House, just through haste and poor planning.

'You jaspers never did think no better than new born newts,' he said with a growl in his voice. 'You don't understand that bein' tight-mouthed is as natural to any desert rat as is breathin'. They'd rather croak six times than tell a body where his hole in the ground might be.'

'She's a desert rat?' Moe Archer queried without thinking.

'So, she's got curvy hips and ruby lips,' Claggett growled. 'So, she's smart enough to come to town and get gone with their supplies every so often, so don't it stand to reason that she must be as much a crafty desert rat as any raggedy-arsed old cactus eater you ever seen?'

'Sorry, Luke,' Archer muttered. 'Never figgered it quite that way.'

'Well, it's high time you started — all

of you,' Claggett chided. Then, satisfied that at last he now had them all utilizing what grey matter the Big House had left them with, he lowered his voice and spoke with authority around his fat black stogie.

'It's plain to me that what we gotta do is just keep watch for this here jade, boys . . . then when she leaves, we follow.'

'Wouldn't she likely be on the lookout for somethin' like that, Luke?' asked Archer.

'She'd never see me, I'd make sure of that. But I wouldn't need to keep her in sight.' Ellington made a sweeping gesture with his right hand. 'I can track a bluebird across an empty sky.'

'Well, with any luck you could get your chance to prove that right soon,' said Claggett. 'All right, now hustle out on to the streets and keep your eyes peeled real sharp. Could well be that jade's thinkin' she might be ready to leave any minute now.'

They hurried out. But there was no need for haste. Hours dragged by on leaden feet, but the battered Stolbeck wagon remained out front of the San Paulo Hotel. Sundown saw an impatient Claggett send Archer off to the hotel to find out what the hell was delaying the girl's departure, suspicious of some kind of sly female trickery maybe.

Turned out Amy Stolbeck was visiting with an old friend, the hotel-keeper's daughter. Archer had tracked the two young women down to the haberdashery where he'd sighted the pair trying on new hats in the parlour.

Claggett took the news badly. 'Whoever said women were strange cattle had it dead to rights!' he snarled. But after getting that off his chest there was nothing to do but settle down to wait and watch some more.

★ ★ ★

It was just turning dark when Shell Dunbar emerged from the San Paulo hotel. He'd slept the hot afternoon away and awoke refreshed. Another long soak in the tub out back and the return of his freshly laundered rig from the Chinese laundry saw him finally emerge from his room ready for anything, but in this case, what he was ready for now was the trail.

He had made the decision to quit town upon awakening. San Paulo had served its purpose. Usually it took him a little more time than this, along with another bottle or two of rye whiskey, to purge himself of the remorse that came in the wake of a gun showdown. But his brief meeting with the lovely girl had somehow convinced him he'd already put it behind him and was ready for the trail.

Yet he still was not certain whether to go looking for a bounty or if he might just drift a spell. He would make a decision on that once on the trail.

He wasn't surprised that the girl kept intruding as he strode along the walk and swung in at the cigar store. He'd caught a glimpse of her on his way up to his room and she'd stared straight through him. He could now grin at the recollection. Strong-minded as well as pretty. Too bad he'd made such a lousy first impression, otherwise he just might have been tempted to stay on and make one last try to get to know her better.

'Two dozen Cuban cigarillos, Lucky,' he said to the lugubrious storekeeper.

'Huh?'

'Cigars.'

'Why didn't you say so?'

Dunbar nodded to himself as the man sighed ponderously and occupied the best part of a minute getting his purchase together, causing him to muse that he might well miss a pair of deep-blue eyes, but he sure as hell wasn't going to miss San Paulo.

Dragging on a fresh stogie, he headed for the livery along the echoing plank-walk.

Sidewalk loafers and front porch loungers eyed him cautiously as he passed by and he glimpsed several of his adversaries from the Crying Shame amongst the citizens out enjoying the soft dusk. He even saw one of the black-bearded man's sidekicks, though the fellow didn't appear to notice him as he stared off intently in the direction of the livery.

Dunbar rubbed his bruised shoulder as he continued on. The roughnecks had done a good job of tossing him out of the saloon, but as things had worked out, they had done him a good turn in hastening his decision to move on.

It was when he reached the last alleyway before the livery, where a buckboard stood, that he heard voices in low argument from the gloom. He had walked on before he realized that one of the voices he'd overheard had been a woman's, and it was a voice he'd recognized.

He propped, frowned, then backed up and squinted down the alleyway. He sighted two silhouettes, one male, the other very definitely female. Moments later he heard Amy Stolbeck say urgently;

'Ten dollars then, Joey. Twice the usual price.'

'Sorry, Miss Amy,' a youthful voice replied. 'But I just ain't got the stomach for it this time. Not with them strangers doggin' you, I don't.'

The girl made to reply when she grew aware of Dunbar standing on the walk. The bounty hunter fingered his hat brim and moved into the gloom of the alley.

'Anything wrong, Miss Amy?'

Her face was a pale oval in the reflected lamplight. Her companion was a skinny youth about seventeen years old.

'Everything is perfectly all right, sir,' she said stiffly, yet Dunbar detected a note of nervousness.

'Didn't sound like it,' Dunbar countered. He nodded at the youth. 'What's going on, kid?'

'Is he one of them, Miss Amy?' the boy asked nervously.

'One of who?' Dunbar demanded. 'Look, you'd better level with me, Miss

Amy. He said something about someone dogging you. What did he mean by that?'

Her eyes scanned his face in the half-light and it seemed to Dunbar that some of the hostility seemed to fade. 'It's really no concern of yours, Mr Dunbar. It's my problem and I'm quite capable of handling it.'

'A problem?' Dunbar persisted. Then he smiled. 'You'd best tell me, Miss Amy, for I'm surely stubborn by nature.'

'I reckon I'd be best gettin' along home, Miss Amy,' the youth said, edging away. 'Sorry I can't help you. Next time, maybe?'

'All right, Joey,' the girl said with a sigh. 'And I understand. It's a lot to ask, considering . . . '

'Considering what?' Dunbar wanted to know as the boy vanished.

'What I was asking him to do, of course,' she said brusquely. Then she shrugged and folded her arms. 'You see, Mr Dunbar, whenever I come to San

Paulo for supplies, I'm always aware that somebody might try to follow me back to the mine — men being what they are. So I arrange for a decoy. The last few times, I've used Joey. He dresses as a girl, wearing a wig, and drives off fast along the old Ring trail while I take our second buckboard and leave town at exactly the same time by a back street and drive off in the opposite direction. I don't know for certain if anybody ever followed Joey, but I do know I was never followed home. Satisfied?'

'Smart,' Dunbar conceded. 'But why wouldn't he go along with you tonight?'

'You really are very nosy.'

'And stubborn. Don't forget that.'

'Just who are you, sir? You look very different tonight from this afternoon.'

'I'm a friend, lady. I want you to believe that. I work for the law.'

'You're a lawman?' Her tone was incredulous.

'Not exactly that. But what's important is that I can help you if you let me.'

58

'Why should you?'

'You're the prettiest woman I ever saw.'

He was astonished to hear himself say that — tight-lipped Shell Dunbar. The girl appeared taken aback for a moment. But then she smiled.

'Thank you,' she said simply. 'Now, I really must go.'

He placed a restraining hand on her arm as she made to step by.

'Let me help you,' he said. 'That boy was scared. He claims someone was dogging you. Who is it?'

She hesitated, then spoke with some resignation. 'I've had the feeling that four strangers have been keeping watch on me all afternoon.'

'What do they look like?'

She described the men and it was plain they were the four he'd tangled with at the Crying Shame Saloon with indifferent success.

He said,' You're dead sure about this?' Then immediately recalled the hardcase on the sidewalk. He nodded before she could reply. 'Yeah . . . maybe you could be right about that. Well, I agree that bunch looks like trouble, right enough. Just could be they're outlaws of some breed.'

She looked apprehensive. 'Do you really think so?'

'Well, I've known my share of that breed and they've got the look.' Dunbar fell thoughtfully silent for the moment. Gazing out into the street, he saw that the buckboard drawn up at the alleymouth was the girl's. Then he saw that the objects she was toting over her arm were in fact a dress and a wig, the disguise for the reluctant Joey.

He smiled. Most of what he did was dangerous, with hard money and maintenance of the law his incentives, with violence and sometimes sudden death the natural outcomes.

He was realizing it was a long time since he'd done something just for the hell of it, or to maybe help somebody out of a fix. The notion fast building up in his mind now was not without its appealing side. To help this fine-looking woman and maybe at the same time leave Blackbeard and his hard-noses with egg on their faces, added up to a prospect with more than a little appeal.

'Miss Amy,' he said impulsively, 'I figured I'd used up just about every trick in the book to fool hardcases out to give me a hard time, but maybe that's not quite so.'

'I don't understand?'

'Then just listen, ma'am, and tell me how this sounds to you.'

*   *   *

It was some time later when the odd alert citizen on the street glimpsed a shadowy figure slip from the alley, clamber up into the Stolbeck buckboard and whip the mules into a trot.

There was a momentary glimpse of long dark tresses flowing in the wind and a vivid crimson dress such as Moe Archer had seen the Stolbeck woman wearing on quitting the hotel.

By the time the buckboard had

wheeled from sight along the old Ring trail that led east out of town, four horsemen were seen wheeling their mounts away from the hitchrack at the Crying Shame Saloon.

From the far end of the alley, Amy Stolbeck, decked out in levis and shirt and with her supplies piled high in the second wagon she kept at the livery for this very type of situation, glimpsed the four strangers lope by.

With a satisfied nod, she slapped the mules into a trot, swung around Dockerty's barn, then took the trail towards the desert just as the moon was coming up.

The disguised Dunbar covered two swift miles along the trail before hauling up to water the mules at a tiny stream. With his ears pricked to every slight sound, he picked up the low drumming of hoofbeats backtrail.

With a cheery grin, he slapped the mules and crossed the stream and climbed the rise beyond. Amy had told him the Ring trail was some ten miles long, circling out past the old Lucky Cuss Mine before curving around and running back to town.

He calculated he should be back in San Paulo, mounted up and be long gone before the hardcases ended up back where they started from, and realized they'd been fooled.

But so much for the best laid plans of mice and men.

One mile south of the creek, the front offside wheel hit a sharp ditch and splintered the axle. Escaping with just a shaking, Dunbar inspected the damage and saw straight off there was no hope of making the wagon roadworthy again in the short time he might have before trouble caught up with him. So, shucking off wig and skirt, he unharnessed the mules, mounted one and, leading the other, took off fast.

It was some time before the outlaws reached the wrecked wagon.

They puzzled for a time over the dress and wig, but it wasn't until they saw that the crates in the wagon were empty that the nickel dropped, and Luke Claggert's tough face was an ugly sight to see as he led them away at a hard gallop on the trail of the missing mules.

Dunbar gave them a run for their money. Yet he was still several miles from town when the riders showed up behind, the long legs and stamina of their big horses ensuring they covered two yards to his mules' one.

'Mebbe not quite as simple as you figured, bounty hunter,' Dunbar muttered to himself and, slipping the second mule loose, jerked rein and took to the brush.

But the Claggett bunch had played this game before. They picked up his trail and for several long miles they pushed him hard through the brush country and eventually closed in close enough to identify him.

'Jumped up Judas from Joliet!' Archer shouted above the drumbeat of hoofs. 'It's that loud mouth sonofa from the saloon!'

Instantly Claggett jerked up his rifle and touched off a shot, the bullet screaming off rock ten feet to Dunbar's right. 'Haul up, you bastard!' he roared. Then fired again.

Teeth gritted and jaws locked, Dunbar leaned low over the mule's sweating neck and sent it at a stumbling run for the timberline ahead. And he was raging. Outlaws! He'd read their brand right from the jump. Only that breed of scum would open up on a man that way, and he knew that had not Wagoner's Switch been so fresh in his mind, he might have elected to stand and make a fight of it.

But he didn't want more dead men, he told himself. He'd never killed willingly or easily, regardless of the name he'd been tagged with.

The timber loomed close now as he reflected that the prime objective had been achieved. Amy Solbeck would have made good her run-out, and might count herself damned lucky to shake a bunch as mean as this one. If he made the timber ahead, he should be able to lose them. If he made the timber . . .

His pursuers were bent low over their mounts' necks, riding hands and heels now in their desperation to get to him before he made cover. A quick glance over his shoulder showed the hook-beaked rannie had dropped back to line up a rifle shot.

A swift jerk on the reins chopped the mule sharply to the left. The rifle crashed, sharp and hard, the slug whistling over the mule's rump to smack a big yellow boulder and go screaming upwards in a howling ricochet.

Dunbar could still hear the echoing rumble of the shot as the first trees closed about him, that sound followed hard by the black-bearded *hombre*'s frustrated shout.

He plunged headlong downslope through dappled moonshadows, holding the mule to a zig-zagging course as he angled for that steep-faced ridge he'd sighted first from beyond the jack pines.

The hoofbeats of the pursuers were muffled now by pine needles — they couldn't fire because of the trees. Froth streamed from the mule's gaping jaws now and its barrel chest heaved like a bellows. But the beast only had to cover another fifty yuards and the ridge loomed.

'Thanks, pard,' Dunbar grunted, and hit the ground running.

'Yonder he goes!' hollered a big voice. 'The varmint's afoot now, boys!'

But this varmint now held his long-barrelled Peacemaker in his fist. Relief gave way to the anger that worked in his chest as he bounded up that steep slope. His light-hearted scheme to draw these sons of bitches away from San Paulo was deteriorating into a grim matter of life or death. He knew if they made it impossible for him to escape he would make a stand and a lot of people were going to bleed.

And Shell Dunbar wasn't planning on being one of them.

His breath burning in his lungs and

with low branches whipping across his face, he crested the ridge a short time later just as a lean rider on a grey pony burst into the open a hundred yards behind. The man's weapon came up and Dunbar flung himself headlong, tumbling down the far slope as the slug powdered the crown of a boulder between his flying heels.

Hauling himself erect and sucking in a huge breath, he plunged on downhill through a vine-choked gulch, but then got a second wind and went racing up the far slope like a startled coyote fleeing from a relay of hound dogs.

He was making time yet knew inside that if he had the chance to wager on the outcome of this chase, he wouldn't risk a silver dollar on Shell Dunbar right now.

4

Grit and Gunsmoke

The riders were falling behind!

Dunbar had just a handful of seconds to draw comfort from that fact before Blackbeard's huge voice sounded again.

'Git off and git after him. He cain't outrun us all, b'God!'

For a long moment bitterness and exhaustion threatened to overcome the sweating bounty man. But no longer than that. Forcing a grim smile, he sucked in a huge lungful of mountain air, thumped his chest with clenched fist, then went shouldering on through the thick brush. It wasn't over — not by a long shot.

The country here was both steep and heavily wooded, much like the West Texas hill country where he'd hunted his first outlaws — the notorious Bick gang, who'd murdered the sheriff in his hometown of Clay. This was his kind of land. His ally, not his enemy.

Another mile and he began to slow. But not from exhaustion or lack of will to continue. Something was hardening inside him as he loped beneath a giant sentinel pine which thrust its gaunt fingers high into the sky.

The lope cut back to a swift walk, which over the next quarter-mile dropped back to almost a saunter.

Behind, he heard an excited yip — they thought he was running out of wind or courage, maybe both.

He knew different, and the Shell Dunbar who finally halted and took cover in a high cluster of rocks, then fingered his hat back from a sweating brow, was a very different man from the almost easy-going Dunbar they'd first tagged.

'You can back off or start dying, hardcases! The choice is yours!'

His voice boomed out, echoing off the cliffs. For a moment all was still.

Then he heard them start in yelling again, firing each other up in the belief that he'd run empty on breath and courage, that, in fact, he'd run his race.

And now he could see them forcing their way uphill through the timber with new energy, leg-weary yet almost swaggering at the anticipation of victory.

The redhead was leading the pack as they crossed a clearing. Dunbar didn't hesitate. Rifle at shoulder, he took a quick, sure bead and squeezed trigger.

His bullet slammed the man's shoulder with the impact of a pile driver, sending him tumbling backwards with his rifle going one way and his sorry hat the other. He continued rolling until he dropped from sight.

Silence.

The stillness held for several minutes until the voice he recognized as Blackbeard's boomed angrily up the slope. 'You busted up a good man, Dunbar. Ain't no way you're gonna walk away from this now.'

An onlooker would have found Dunbar's reaction surprising. He leaned his back against a trunk and smiled in relief, buoyed now by the old fighter's adage: 'When they start talking it means they've stopped fighting.'

So it proved when some quarter hour later he heard the sounds that told him the enemy was shifting ground — retreating.

There followed a tirade of cussing and threatening, yet all the while the voices were growing fainter, until a voice he recognized as Blackbeard's sounded startlingly closer.

'You're on borrowed time, pilgrim. I'll peg your dirty hide out to dry iffen it takes from now to Thanksgivin'! Believe that if you've ever believed anythin'!'

That was the last seen or heard of the pack, and Dunbar felt easy enough to get moving just a short time later. He made his way deeper into the rough country for a spell, took up another vantage spot — just in case. But soon he was walking freely again, stepping out westward now, refreshed and easy in himself the way it always was when a man beat the odds. He hated to walk as a rule, but was glad to do so here to rid himself of the very last traces of his hard-drinking spree in San Paulo.

He finally came to the last butte he'd marked earlier. Holstering his six-shooter, he climbed thirty feet up the uneven flank to see the plains country unfolding before his gaze. Miles west-ward, the dim lights of San Paulo lay scattered about like beads against the dun-coloured flats. From here he could make out the trace of the Ring trail where it swung away from the town on the north-east side, and further on, where it curved back east.

A thin patina of dust hung over the southern trail, and focusing sharply, he eventually made out the four tiny figures of the horsemen making their way back to town.

Only then did he totally relax. Stretching out with his back against a rock, he smiled broadly. It had been a little touch-and-go for a time back there, and considering the determination and calibre of his pursuers, he supposed he was lucky to come out of the scrape with just a few scratches and bruises.

He sobered as he reflected on that bunch now. His bounty hunter's instincts had warned him from the outset that they might well be outlaws from the first moment they'd come tramping into the Crying Shame Saloon, and in the light of recent events over the past couple of hours, suspicion had hardened into certainty.

He would now wager good money that those four hardfaces dominated Wanted dodgers some place, maybe even many places. Maybe if he was to wire descriptions through to the Rangers at the county law office he might strike pay dirt, then have a solid, cash-money reason to go after them.

He was, after all, a bounty hunter by trade.

Normally the scent of a good manhunt could be guaranteed to command Shell Dunbar's full attention. Not so now. For some reason he found his focus lapsing. Replacing Blackbeard and his running dogs now was a soft oval face framed by raven-black hair and eyes as blue as a whole range of Texas prairie flowers.

He closed his eyes and saw her as he'd done last in that alley, smiling at the ridiculous sight he'd presented in a dress many sizes too small and a shoulder-length black wig.

He attempted to laugh off the very notion that any female could captivate Shell Dunbar, but the smile just wouldn't come. Instead, he felt a strange ache some place that had its core in a bounty hunter's loneliness, something that was a secret part of his dangerous life he shared with nobody.

He conjured up images of other girls in other places and knew none had ever aroused in him more than a passing interest. Men of the gun traditionally

and wisely rarely formed lasting attach-
ments. Compulsively, defiantly, they
walked the razor's edge largely alone.

Yet there was no denying that the
ache was there, while the thought that
he wouldn't see her again was almost
like pain.

He opened his eyes and rose with an
impatient grunt. If this was the best he
could do resting up, he would be better
off walking.

With the country rough and broken
to the west of the butte, he chose to
work his way back the way he'd come,
cut the Ring trail some place then
follow it back to San Paulo.

He calculated the walk could occupy
two to three hours, plenty of time for a
bunch of hardcases to take on a bellyful
of whiskey and go to sleep. He knew
now he wouldn't waste time wiring
around for information on the bunch's
movements, if known. Instead he would
saddle up and ride and forget San
Paulo and everybody in it just as fast as
he could.

A chill wind blew in from the desert as the lone walker reached the cross trail and struck off westward. He kept a sharp watch in the hope of maybe sighting one of the mules, but with no luck.

He trudged along doggedly, a man alone, and one who just hated to walk. At last the weariness caught up with him as it must. It had been a mighty big day in more ways than one, and San Paulo was still a long way off. He came to a creek which he guessed had to be the same one he'd crossed further north in the buckboard. Stripping off his shirt, he immersed himself to the waist. He drank to excess, swallowing down great draughts, until he'd had more than his fill. After repeatedly soaking his head in the deliciously cold water, he smiled with simple animal pleasure, then laughed out loud.

It was only when he fell totally silent again that he heard it. From somewhere beyond the west bluffs came the steady sound of hoofs, the creak of an axle.

Dunbar was up and out and into the brush in a flash, the Peacemaker cocked and ready in his fist. The sounds swelled and shortly the big-eared heads of two mules showed above the crest in the trail. Taking sight, he waited, as immobile and dangerous as a hungry puma.

Abruptly the buckboard came lurching into full view, a battered old cart with a slender figure perched upon the high-sprung driver's seat.

Slowly he lowered the revolver and, wide-eyed, stepped from cover.

'Miss Amy, what the tarnal are you doing out here in the middle of the night?'

'Mr Dunbar?' Her voice sounded small in the night, a child's voice.

Dunbar laughed as he scooped up his shirt and waded across the stream with moonlight shimmering on his naked torso. 'It's me right enough, Miss Amy. But what the tarnal are you doing out here?'

The girl dragged the mules to a halt

on the downslope and pressed a hand to her breast. 'Oh, I'm so relieved to see you, Mr Dunbar. What on earth was all that shooting earlier, do you know?'

'You heard it?' he asked, pulling on his shirt.

She nodded, gesturing southward. 'Our trail runs a couple of miles south of the Ring Trail until reaching the desert. I imagined what I heard at first to be thunder, but when I finally halted I realized . . . ' She swallowed then added, 'Are you quite sure you're not hurt?'

He almost said, 'I should be sure.' But something held him back. He wanted to impress, not offend. His record with women was patchy at best, due to his sometime habit of talking without thinking. He smiled. 'Well, I did get marked up some earlier, I'll allow. Matter of fact, I don't feel all that chipper right now, er, miss.'

Smartly knotting her reins around the whip socket, Amy climbed over the seat and rummaged in the supplies to produce a flask of whiskey. Dunbar drew the cork for her and took a pull on the spirits, swallowed then waited for the good inner warmth to spread. Then he took another, smaller sip and proceeeded to explain what had happened.

Perched upon the back of the seat, Amy listened wide-eyed. When he was through, she said, 'Oh, I feel terrible, Mr Dunbar. I had no idea that you really — Well, as I said earlier, there has never been any serious trouble before whenever Joey acted as decoy for me. But to think those awful men actually tried to kill you!'

'Well, trying and succeeding are two different things, I reckon. But I've got to say I reckon it was right brave of you to come looking back here after hearing those guns, never knowing what you might run into. Right brave.'

'Surely it was the least anybody could do?'

'Not to my way of thinking.'

She studied him silently for a

moment, then glanced westwards. 'Are you quite sure those gunmen returned to town?'

He nodded. 'Sure.'

'Do you intend going back to San Paulo now?'

His face blanked. He might have forgotten the girl with the beautiful face had he not seen her again, he reflected. But meeting her again all the way out here at the end of several tough and highly dangerous hours, under a fat moon and with a burbling river in the background . . . well, he was no longer dead certain what he should tell her.

He took a gamble and said, 'Guess I've got no choice.'

'What do you plan to do when you get there?'

'Why, get my horse and ride — I guess.'

'You don't seem certain.'

'Well, considering the shape I'm in, along with the chance that those hellions might be sitting up waiting for me to show up through the tall grass, I guess I can't be sure how going back might play out . . . '

He let his voice fade and shrugged, allowed his shoulders to sag. He was playing an unfamiliar game here, unsure what form it might take, only knowing he didn't want to say goodbye again so soon.

The girl didn't speak for a long minute. While staring across the river he was aware of her looking him up and down, measuring him. He knew she regarded him as trouble, so he did his best to appear reassuring.

The creek gurgled and one of the mules lowered its head to drink and the moonlight formed a halo around Amy Stolbeck's glossy dark hair.

'Well, miss,' he sighed at length, 'I guess we aren't going to boil any beans sitting around here, so — '

'I feel you should go back with me.'

'Huh?'

'It just wouldn't feel right,' she stated firmly, sliding across to the driver's side. 'You risked your life for me tonight and very nearly lost it. You are tired and in danger and the least I can do is see you safely back and then ensure you are safe and rested.'

'Are you talking about taking me to the mine?'

She nodded briskly. 'It's the only place you'd be safe. Of course, Pa won't like it, but I can handle him. Now, you'd better climb up and we'll get under way. We can't be sure those awful men won't come back.'

'This is mighty caring of you, ma'am.'

'Tell me about it later. Please get up, Mr Dunbar.'

'On one condition.'

She frowned. 'What's that?'

'That you start calling me Shell.'

She looked annoyed. 'Do please hurry.'

'Shell.'

'All right — Shell!'

Dunbar smiled and swung up, forgetting for the moment he was supposed to be poorly. So, as he sat, he pressed a hand to his ribs and grimaced. 'Mighty grateful, Miss Amy,' he panted. 'The way I'm feeling right now I'm not sure I'd have made it back to town anyway.'

'You'll be just fine, Shell,' she promised warmly, and for a moment Dunbar hated himself for his small deception. But only for a moment. Studying her profile as she expertly wheeled the team and sent them back along the trail, he realized he would have been prepared to spin every black lie in the book just to buggy-ride with Amy Stolbeck beneath a brilliant Texas moon.

It felt almost romantic and may have even been so had he felt relaxed enough to take hand off gun handle for one moment during the eight-mile run across country to the hidden and secret Overman Mine.

But he didn't.

★ ★ ★

Slumped in a cane-bottomed rocker in the shade of the hotel porch, Luke Claggett watched San Paulo sourly in the morning.

There were few on the streets as yet. A prospector with a beard like a bird's nest sat on the bench of the boarded-up assay office and a white-aproned bartender desultorily swept the front porch of the Crying Shame with a whisk broom. A Double Cross wagon was drawn up alongside the feed and grain store and two men carried out plump sacks of grain to stack in the wagon bed.

The hardcase stretched and sighed heavily. In the dining-room behind him he could hear the tinny clink and clatter of dishes as the hotel-keeper's skinny daughter laid the places.

It was a pleasant, peaceful sound which failed to cheer Luke Claggett any at all.

He leaned forward to watch a wino slouch by, eyeing the man closely just in case he should reveal by his glance that he knew how Claggett had been made to look a fool in public last night. But luckily the derelict had but one thing on his mind today and kept plodding on by with his gaze fixed with an alcoholic's intensity on the batwings of the saloon, leaving Claggett to slump back in his chair.

He lighted a stogie and had half-smoked it by the time Moe Archer and Jimmy Ellington emerged from the Crying Shame and started across the street. Claggett studied them closely. They appeared sober, which was just as well. He'd sent them across there to get information, not drink.

The hardcases sat down on the porch and made their report.

Nobody knew for sure if old man Stolbeck had struck it rich out in the Seven Sisters, Archer stated, yet most folks believed he had. They did know for sure that Rooney Stolbeck was mighty tight-fisted, however, and considered himself a cut above the general run. The Stolbecks had come to the

Seven Sisters from the East the year before and there was a rumour that the girl had been engaged to marry the son of a famous man.

'What a load of hogwash,' was Claggett's response. 'I sent you for information and you fetch me a passel of back-fence gossip. Would it matter a bullet in the backside if the jade was married to the king of New Orleans? What good is this henscratch to me?'

The two hardcases exchanged a glance. Luke was mighty touchy today, no mistake, they realized. But they were hardly surprised by this, for by nature Claggett bitterly hated to lose.

Ellington twisted a cigarette into shape and delivered some further information, unpalatable though it might be.

The Stolbeck's secret Overman Mine was believed to be a long way out in the desert, he affirmed. Nobody knew even the general location, although there were any number of locals who'd made attempts to find it. The girl only ever came to town every couple of months and was very crafty when it came to covering her tracks.

'Tell me somethin' I don't know,' Claggett grunted.

Moe Archer proceeded to do just that. He'd heard at the saloon that Dunbar had received a wire yesterday from a Texas Ranger. The lawman had asked Dunbar to contact him, and he'd done so, wiring back that the Ranger should 'forget it'.

There was no brusque comment from Claggett this time, for the very suggestion that Dunbar might be connected with the law seemed to offer some explanation for that hard-nose's behaviour. Claggett had dubbed Dunbar a coward when he backed down in front of a gun at the saloon, yet his actions out in the hills the previous night had proved beyond any doubt that Amy Stolbeck's new friend was anything but yellow.

But the way Claggett saw it, the possibility that Dunbar could be law was just another good reason to nail him. And this brought him back to hard-edged reality. Before you got to nail up a skunk skin on your barn door, first, you had to catch your skunk.

Dunbar had not returned from San Paulo. His horse was still at the livery stables.

Claggett let his gaze drift southwards, beyond the raddled hills and buttes to where the desert's edge lay like a shimmering bar on the horizon. His top lip twitched. There had to be gold out there, otherwise what were those folks doing at the Seven Sisters? That sure wasn't the kind of place a man would live just for the sake of his health.

Only one thing for it. It was high time he stopped talking and settled down to some serious thinking.

5

Lure of Gold

The Overman Mine headquarters wasn't visible until you were almost on top of it. The buildings stood in a deep canyon shielded by a high line of brush.

Amy smiled at Dunbar's evident surprise as she guided the buckboard through a maze of brush and the canyon suddenly opened up before them.

Dunbar pivoted in his seat and stared backtrail. He saw that their tracks showed clearly behind. He looked a question at the girl, who smiled again.

'The wind rises every night as regular as clockwork, Shell,' she explained. 'By morning there won't be a trace of a track left.'

Dunbar nodded, beginning to understand just how it was that the Stolbecks had managed to keep their secret for so long. Here, ten miles out in the desert by his estimation, the mine was located where a man would have to stumble upon it by accident to find it, and then there was that dependable night breeze to sweep away any sign which might be left coming or going.

He smiled wonderingly and thought there was small wonder the Stolbecks had managed to survive and thrive for so long.

The trail angled sharply downwards, curving past a giant slab of stone then straightened out as the canyon widened. The house stood directly ahead surrounded by outbuildings, a corral and a chicken run. A hundred yards beyond the buildings, partly concealed by brush, stood the yawning mouth of the mine and a massive pile of tailings. Standing by the rig in the hot sun gazing around at the mine workings with the girl at his side, Dunbar was both intrigued and impressed. But the same did not apply to the angry man watching them over the sights of a

Henry Big Fifty rifle.

Rooney Stolbeck was so enraged by what he was seeing that he found it impossible to keep his Big Fifty rifle steady as he crouched behind the chicken coop, mouthing curses like a muleskinner. His anger was in no way appeased when his daughter waved a cheerful greeting on suddenly spotting the crown of his derby hat and the wink of sunlight on gun barrel.

'Hello, Pa! Come on out and meet Shell Dunbar!'

After what seemed a long time, Rooney emerged from cover, five feet nothing of quivering outrage dwarfed by the huge weapon in his hands. Even in working garb Amy's father managed to appear almost elegant, surely a rare characteristic for anyone associated with mining.

'And what the living hell is this about?' the little man wanted to know.

'I just told you, Pa. Shell Dunbar is a friend we can trust.'

'Friend?' The father's face, mottled

crimson now, was distinguished by a silver moustache and whiskers, completing the picture of a man of style and quality who'd fallen on hard times. 'We don't have any friends as you damn well know, girl. All we have surrounding us here are dirty, no-good sons of bitches who would kill their own mothers to get their thieving hands on what belongs to us.'

'That will be enough of that foolish carry-on and bad language, Pa,' Amy reproved, and Dunbar had his first hint that fiesty Rooney Stolbeck might not have things entirely his own way out here in the boondocks. 'Now, kindly put that ridiculous weapon away and come over here and shake hands with Shell. I mean now, Father!'

The little man immediately lowered the piece and came stomping across to them, but there was no way he was about to shake hands.

'You must be out of your mind, girl. We sweat blood keeping no-goods away from here, yet here you go actually bringing one in. Who is he, and what the hell does he want?'

'I'm a bounty hunter and a friend of your daughter's,' Dunbar said quietly. 'And I've got no interest in your mine.'

'A bounty hunter? You mean you kill men for money?'

Aware of the girl's searching gaze, Dunbar said, 'I work both for the law and with the law at times. I bring in men they can't catch. Mostly I bring them in alive, but if there's no other way I bring them in any way I can.'

He looked at Amy directly, half-expecting to see revulsion in her face. But her expression told him nothing.

'Shell did me a great service in San Paulo, Pa,' she stated calmly, 'and I don't want you to say any more until you hear all about that. And now, we could all use some coffee.'

'Coffee? Glory be to God, I'm the one that needs something hot and strong. And not just coffee either. Did you remember my whiskey, or were you too busy making sheep's eyes at this — '

'Your daughter's been through a rough time,' Dunbar cut him off. 'So why don't you take her advice and hobble your tongue until you've heard the full story. Then you can sound off all you want if you've a mind.' A deliberate pause. 'But you'll treat her civil.'

The older man blinked, reddened, stared appealingly at his daughter but found no help there. So he cursed and whirled away, trailing the butt of the Henry in the dust as he stamped off towards the house.

'Sorry, but I had to set him straight, Amy.'

'It's all right. It will probably do him good.'

He studied her. 'Do you object to the other thing? My work, I mean?'

'I don't judge people by what they do but what they are.'

He smiled, 'I appreciate that. Now, why don't you go inside and settle your pa down while I tote the stuff over to the house.'

'Are you quite sure you're strong enough?' she asked with the hint of a twinkle to suggest she may have been aware of his subterfuge all along.

'Reckon I'll manage,' he said, poker-faced, and watched her head for the house before turning back to the buckboard.

Toting the supplies across to the yard, Dunbar took the opportunity to familiarize himself with the layout. The size and number of the slag piles over by the mine shaft indicated that the Overman operation must be a sizeable one, suggesting Rooney Stolbeck must be a formidable worker despite his small stature.

The outbuildings all had a solid, durable look and the corral that housed four mules was well built.

The house, although basic, was raised in the spacious south-western fashion, with plain walls under a low-pitched roof, a deep gallery across the face and a walkway that ran right through. A runty live oak shaded the western windows and a luxurious vine cascaded from the eaves, screening the far end of the gallery and flinging streamers up to the live oak branches.

In back of the house stood a workshed, some greenery and a pump. Amy had told him her father had found water here first when he came out prospecting, had promptly set up his base then roamed the Seven Sisters for several months before finding traces of colour in this very canyon, almost on the doorstep.

The set-up appeared secure and solid, but lonesome. It wouldn't suit Shell Dunbar, he knew. But then he glanced towards the house wondering if he was dead sure about that.

Amy called from a window as he toted the last crate across. He returned to the well and sluiced off the sweat and finger-combed his hair before going in.

The house was surprisingly spacious with several rooms leading off the walkway. The kitchen was in back where the girl laid out plates of hot biscuits and steaming mugs of coffee on a pinewood table.

Rooney Stolbeck occupied the chair at the head of the table with a bottle before him and his hat hanging off the back of the chair. He still appeared disgruntled, but less so than before.

'Guess I owe you a word of thanks,' he said grudgingly as Dunbar took his place. He nodded to his daughter. 'Amy just told me all about it.'

'Any man would have done the same,' he said.

'Any man, you say? Trouble is, there wouldn't be a real man in that whole crummy town. The backside of Texas, I call it. And I've made up my mind I'm not going to let Amy go back there again after what happened. I'll starve first.'

Shell just nodded and drank his coffee while the girl brought her father up to date on the happenings in town. She was plainly devoted to the old feller, he thought, but looking around the big bare room wondered what kept her out here even so.

His attention was diverted by a daguerrotype on the mantel. It showed a handsome young man smiling in the sun and standing before a huge white house with lofty columns out front. He wondered if there was a brother Amy hadn't mentioned.

'Well,' Rooney said after a brief silence, 'what are your plans, Dunbar?'

Shell had been expecting this. 'I figured to rest up a few days, then move on. That's if that's all right by you.'

'Of course it is,' Amy said, rising. 'You're welcome to stay as long as you like. Isn't that so, Pa?'

'Well, seeing as how you saw fit to bring him out here, I suppose there's nothing to be gained by my kicking him out,' Rooney said testily. 'But I don't hold with freeloading, mister, so if you stay, you'll work just like — '

'Oh, hush, Pa,' Amy chided from the doorway. 'Don't bother the man with that silly talk. He's tired and needs rest.' She flashed a smile at Dunbar as she went out. 'I'll make up a bed in the front room, Shell. It's the coolest room in the house.'

'That's a fine girl you have there, mister,' Dunbar said quietly.

'I don't need you to tell me that. But you're wasting your time, pilgrim.'

Dunbar frowned as Stolbeck rose and put on his hat. 'What's that supposed to mean?'

'Tarnation! You must think a man's blind. Don't you think I notice the way you look at her, hang on to her every word? You're smitten, Mr Bounty Hunter, just like every other young rooster who claps eyes on her.' Rooney grinned maliciously. 'And you got it real bad, right? I saw that the moment I saw you together.'

'You talk crazy.'

'Is that so? Well, why don't you deny it? Go on, say you can't abide the sight of her.'

'You're loco!'

'Can't say it, can you? That proves you're smitten.'

Dunbar scowled hard. 'You talk way too much, old man. And like most old fellers, you talk a heap of rubbish.'

'Do I? I reckon not. But eat your heart out, bucko, for you are simply wasting your time. Less than no chance — that's what you got with my daughter.'

With that he stamped from the room, well pleased with himself, leaving Shell to wonder how the ornery old fool could be so sure of that.

6

The Bad Breed

Shell was awakened next morning by the chirping of birds in the oak outside his window and the grating sounds of Rooney Stolbeck filing an edge on to his shovel out on the gallery.

'Rise and shine!' the miner yelled with excessive gusto as he appeared at the window. 'This here is your banjo and I'm going to see you play it.'

Dunbar stared down at the man stonily, already convinced that Stolbeck was someone easy to dislike. He had a couple of retorts on the tip of his tongue when from somewhere within the house Amy's voice sounded, causing his annoyance to vanish instantly.

'Oh, do hush up and let the man at least get to awaken properly, Pa!'

'Whatever you say, girlie,' Rooney

said with a malicious wink at Shell. Then he grabbed up the shovel again and filed so loudly even the mules in the corral seemed to wince. Dunbar knew he was expected to react, but wouldn't. Instead he went to his room and pulled on his rig before heading for the kitchen. He liked it out here and no mouthy old man was going to put him off — that was for sure.

Breakfast comprised beefsteak and eggs, sunny side up, washed down by generous draughts of coffee. After this the two men left for the mine. Having decided to stay on for a spell at the girl's insistence, Dunbar was determined not to be a burden. Despite the fact that the Stolbecks seemed to have a productive mine, they showed little signs of affluence with only minimum creature comforts to be seen about the place.

Never having worked in a mine before he was surprised by the welcome coolness down in the lamplit shaft. Rooney, revealing a surprisingly muscular body when stripped to the waist, tore into the rock face with his pick, plainly determined to show his guest what a man thirty years his senior could do.

Dunbar took it steadily during the morning stint and Rooney reported to his daughter over lunch that as a worker he was about average.

Yet as the long afternoon wore on Rooney naturally began to slow some while Shell deliberately picked up his work rate. For every wagon load of ore the older man filled, he filled one and a half, and towards dusk was leading Amy's father two-to-one.

He didn't expect this to endear him to Stolbeck, and the man was in a sour and silent mood as they tramped across the canyon for the house just on dusk. Over supper they began discussing the buckboard again and Rooney declared sarcastically that, seeing as their guest now seemed so 'all-fired healthy' he saw no reason why they shouldn't take a couple of mules and some tools and go repair the vehicle and fetch it back.

Amy objected, feeling it might be dangerous for Dunbar to return to San Paulo. But he did not agree. He was willing to go, he insisted, believed there wouldn't be any risk attached to going to the vehicle several miles out of the town. But there were other reasons behind his decision, one of which was that this job of work would delay him having to make a decision as to when he should leave. The two eventually reached agreement and planned to set out later in the cool of the night in order to reach their destination around first light. That would enable the repairs to be made early then get back to the Overman by noon and beat the worst of the day's heat.

Following the meal Rooney went off to the tack room to patch harness, leaving Dunbar and Amy seated on the gallery watching the moon rise over the monolith rock.

Shell was aching from the long day's labour, but it was a good feeling. The night breeze had sprung up and was stirring Amy's dark silky hair upon her shoulders.

Dunbar felt strangely content, yet knew this couldn't last. It never did. Contentment was never a constant in the life of a bounty hunter.

The two talked easily as the moon climbed high and at her request Dunbar revealed some things about himself, touching only lightly on the violent episodes of his life and elaborating on good times.

He was surprised to realize how few of the latter there really were. Looking back over the years it seemed he'd always felt driven restlessly to follow one lonely trail after another, rarely finding the time to sit on moonlit porches with pretty girls.

And thought . . . maybe his life would have been very different had he met someone like this before his work got to rule him the way it did.

Amy freely discussed her life before coming to the Seven Sisters. Her father had been a cattleman in East Texas and she had grown up in an atmosphere of comfortable wealth. This part of her story was dotted with references to splendid parties, carriages and fine horses and schools where girls were taught how to be ladies first and foremost with the academic curriculum very low on the agenda.

She spoke candidly enough, he supposed. But it seemed to him there were blank patches she didn't care to fill in. Occasionally her expression would become grave as though recalling something unpleasant, yet the only really bad incident she touched on was how Rooney had lost his money. Tying on a monumental bender a week after Amy's mother died, Rooney got involved in a high-stake poker game and was cleaned out down to his bedrocks in three hours.

Father and daughter had subsequently headed West to search for gold with nothing more than four mules and a loaded buckboard — the same one which had fallen apart on Dunbar in the hills.

Amy claimed that ever since that card game her father had turned bitter and miserly, and Dunbar reckoned he could understand that.

When Rooney finally finished his banging and clattering about in the tack room and wearily trudged back to the house, Amy went inside to brew more coffee.

The two men sat in silence on the gallery for a spell, eyeing each other warily.

'Y'know, I reckon there's something peculiar about you, mister,' Stolbeck said abruptly.

'Why, that's exactly what I was thinking about you.'

'Don't bandy words with me, sonny. So, how come you ain't asked me anything about my mine?'

'What's to know?'

'That there is a gold mine, mister, and you and me have been digging out ore-body with those little gold flecks in it. So how come you haven't tried to find out how much I've taken out, or where I've got it stashed?'

'I told you when I came. I'm not interested in gold.'

'Every man that ever breathed is interested in the yellow stuff. If a man says otherwise then he isn't telling the truth.'

Dunbar stiffened. 'Don't call me a liar, old man!'

Stolbeck put his hands up placatingly.

'All right, all right, no need to get your dander up. But just so you don't start getting curious about my stash, I might as well tell you, there isn't one. Sure, I found plenty here in the early days. But I shipped it all back East to pay off some big gambling debts and since the main lode ran out I've barely made foodstore money.'

'No concern of mine.'

'But just on account I'm poor doesn't mean I don't have prospects.' Stolbeck jerked a gnarled thumb over his shoulder. 'That goes for Amy too. She was born to quality and she will have it again — all of it. She is a country mile too good for the likes of you — nothing personal you understand?'

Shell grinned. He was slowly growing accustomed to the man's abrasiveness.

'None taken. Only thing, I reckon any woman over the age of twenty-one has the right to make her own decisions . . . about anything or anyone.'

'She's made hers.'

'Meaning?'

'Meaning, I've said all I mean to.'

They had been silent for a time after that before Amy came out. 'Have you two been squabbling again?' she asked, placing her tray on a low table.

'Your pa's an easy man to squabble with,' Dunbar said easily.

'They don't come any easier, do they, Pa?' the girl laughed, patting Stolbeck's cheek affectionately.

'Hummphh!' snorted Rooney, and attacked the hot biscuits like a starving man.

Soon after, Dunbar took a nap and

Amy awakened him with a light knock at midnight. Dressing quickly, he pulled on one of Rooney's old jackets against the chill and went outside to ready the mules. Stolbeck had packed a tool kit for him which he now strapped on to one mule, saddled the other, and was ready to pull out.

'Are you quite sure you won't have any trouble finding the way, Shell?' Amy asked when he led the animals across to the house.

'Memorizing trails is part of my trade, Amy.'

'You'll take care, then?'

'Surely. Wish me luck?'

'Of course.'

'I mean really wish me luck.'

'I don't understand.'

He came slowly up the steps, taking off his hat. He stood close to her and she looked up at him uncertainly. Then he drew her to him and kissed her. For a moment she resisted, but only for a moment. The embrace held until she broke away breathlessly, eyes wide, her hand to her breast.

Then without a word, she turned and vanished inside.

The desert winds moaned low and the vines seemed to whisper secrets as Dunbar turned away slowly to descend the steps. He touched fingers to his mouth as he gigged the mules forward.

He'd travelled but a few yards when Rooney appeared, coming round the side of the house.

'Forget something?' Shell queried, drawing rein.

'Mebbe. I got to thinking that if you changed your mind about coming back here you could leave the mules and rig in town at the livery for me to pick up.'

'I'll be back.'

'Maybe it would be best if you just kept going.'

Shell's eyes narrowed. 'You saw what happened, then?'

'You're just taking advantage of her loneliness,' Rooney accused. 'You don't understand what she's been through.' His head bobbed, 'Yeah, reckon it would be better all round if you just kept going, mister.'

Dunbar's jaw set hard. 'I'll quit if she tells me to, old man, not before.'

'You're not right for her. She'll wed well when she gets around to it, after I strike the seams again and when — ' There was more but Dunbar didn't hear as he slapped the mules into a shambling run and headed for the rim.

'I'll go when she tells me to!' he repeated into the teeth of the wind, showing the same resolve that marked his life along the outlaw trails. 'Not before . . . '

★ ★ ★

Moe Archer came awake with a stiff neck and the sound of distant tapping in his ears.

For some time the outlaw lay motionless in his blankets staring up at the branches of the pine tree silhouetted against the lemon light of early morning. He'd not meant to doze off when he'd climbed under the Fort Lincoln blanket for warmth, but he had and now it was several hours later.

Must have been the whiskey he'd brought with him to help ward off the chill during the long night hours.

Then he remembered. He sat up with a start and reached for his .45 before going off to peer over the rock ledge.

The shelf where Archer had spent last night, and Jimmy Ellington the night before, jutted out from the flank of a pine-clothed hillside on the south side of the Ring Trail. Directly below at a distance of some two hundred feet was the buckboard Dunbar had crashed two nights back.

With mist tatters clinging to the trail the buckboard was barely visible.

Archer knuckled the sleep from his eyes. He had not supported the notion that Rooney Stolbeck might make a try to retrieve his buckboard — but there was surely activity going on below right now. And whoever it was down there, was starting in hammering again.

As the light strengthened to penetrate the mist he made out the figure of a man crouched down by the broken front wheel. The buckboard had been braced upon a log and the man was working with sureness yet without haste.

Suddenly the man turned and Archer caught a momentary glimpse of a youthful, saddle-brown face and wide shoulders.

Dunbar!

He remained frozen until he heard the tapping begin again, cautiously lifted his head. He was grinning as he watched the tall figure rise and return to the buckboard for another tool.

Next instant, Archer was gone.

He'd tethered his horse some distance away, but determined not to risk being heard now, he led the animal off quietly for a hundred yards before swinging up.

Then he pointed its nose towards San Paulo and used his spurs.

★ ★ ★

Mid-morning and already blasting hot on the Seven Sisters Desert.

Shell Dunbar studied the mules' sweating backs, then screwed up his eyes as he stared ahead. He recalled that giant saguaro cactus growing out from the base of a twisted talus pile. He made some calculations and figured he was at least halfway home and should raise the canyon around noon.

So the buckboard rolled on, a tiny speck of life like some ungainly insect crawling across the yellow earth. Behind lay featureless plains, ahead a sun-stricken sweep of desert country sparsely dotted with greasewood, mesquite and towering barrel cacti which marched away into the smoky-brown haze that blurred the horizon.

Raddled hills rose far to the east, stippled with spiny cactus.

To the right spread a vast domain of coloured dunes and whispering sand, white beds of alkali and silt. Beyond lay wind-ploughed canyons and the dusty ridges which climbed into tablelands which finally moulded into a range of hills that chopped like fish teeth into a brassy sky.

Badlands.

Passing through the shade flung by a towering butte the rider swivelled to look backtrail. Nothing but heat haze, glare and endless distances. He turned to the way ahead, lit a fresh cigarillo and watched the desert.

He acknowledged that despite its brutal harshness and brain-boiling temperatures, the desert on days like this possessed a kind of raw beauty. And thought — maybe if a man was smart enough to avoid trouble he might find it uncomplicated out here, even agreeable.

You could do worse than embrace the desert, he mused, but only if you had someone to share its solitude and silences.

Times like this Dunbar tended to reflect upon his dangerous profession.

He'd always been dedicated to the law, took great pride in the numbers of killers and thieves he'd either had jugged or hanged. And wondered — should he ever come to quitting — would he be able to hang up the Peacemakers and leave the responsibility of running down the mad dogs to others?

This was something to ponder as the burning miles flowed beneath the rig. When he eventually reached the canyon and sighted Amy she ran to the mine to fetch her father while he made his way on down. And though Rooney appeared grouchy and cantankerous when Dunbar finally wheeled in, he was plainly very pleased to see his buckboard again.

The miner even offered a grudging compliment as he examined the patched-up wheel.

'Not bad for a rush job, I suppose,' he opined. Then straightening he patted the splashboard and actually grinned. 'This here's the rig that brought me and Amy West, you know. I'd sure have hated to lose it.' He sobered. 'Have any trouble?'

'None.'

'Beat?'

'Some, I reckon.'

'Come on inside,' Amy said. 'I've fixed some lemonade.'

Shell looked directly at the girl and it seemed her eyes shone a little brighter as she led the way for the house, and for a moment he wanted to believe that glance meant something special.

But once inside the cool kitchen she seemed to only have eyes for that handsome man in the picture on the wall he didn't want to ask about.

★ ★ ★

'Had an old uncle once who was a desert rat,' Jack Lomas informed. He paused to spit, then continued. 'Everybody said he was loco and I reckon that was nothin' but the simple truth.'

'Are you tryin' to tell us somethin', Jack?' Moe Archer grinned, swabbing sweat from his brow with his sleeve.

'Only that I reckon any white man who goes off into the desert, no matter what the reason, is crazy as a barrelful of loons.'

'Loons never ever get to be rich, Lomas,' growled Jimmy Ellington. The killer was also in good spirits despite the heat of the slow desert crossing beneath a searing sun. They were hunters on a scent and the scent was strong.

'They never get to see their mortal remains blisterin' and bleachin' on some fool stretch of land that God forgot, neither,' Lomas countered.

Ellington winked across at Archer. 'What do you reckon, Moe? Do you figure Jack would have such a mortal set on this here desert if you hadn't told him that Dunbar's out there some place with the rich folks now?'

'Hard to say,' Archer replied. 'How's your top-knot, Jack? Growed any new hair recent?'

'All right, leave him be,' Claggett said from up front, causing Archer and Ellington to stare at him in surprise. Big Luke must be feeling chipper to tolerate that kind of talk, they figured.

This was true.

Claggett was riding high and every time he looked down at the wagon tracks stretching ahead of him, he felt even better.

The killer had encountered opposition when he first insisted on maintaining a round-the-clock watch on the damaged Stolbeck wagon out on the Ring trail, but Archer's sighting of Dunbar that morning had bolstered his theory as well as offering the promise of a big killing.

They rode in silence for a mile, then paused to rest briefly in the shadow of a rock while Ellington scouted ahead. Claggett was taking no risk of blundering on to the mine. He intended to find it, study the layout, then make his plans unhurriedly and with attention to detail. He knew this caution wouldn't be necessary but for Dunbar. Having tangled with the man once he was not prepared to take any fool chances.

Of course, Dunbar would have to go

eventually, he mused as he watched Ellington coming in. Dunbar was dangerous and the only way to deal with that breed was with a bullet. But the old man and the girl? Well, their prospects of survival would depend entirely on how quickly they revealed the whereabouts of the cache. Claggett prided himself on not being a vindictive man. If they told him where the gold was and treated him with respect, he might go easy on them.

Might.

Ellington reported back that he'd seen nothing ahead but more desert. So everybody took another drink and rode out beneath the punishing sun once more.

Tension mounted as slow miles drifted behind, and even Lomas quit griping. By now they were interpreting everything Stolbeck did and said as proof that the man was acting real miserly just to convince the world he was flat busted. They'd come to believe he'd likely made enough to set them all up in luxury for the rest of their lives.

Another mile passed before Ellington abruptly called a halt and gestured ahead. At first the others saw nothing but a long line of brush with a gaunt white cliff raising behind. But when they concentrated and narrowed their eyes they finally made out what the hawk-eyed Ellington had sighted instantly — a low thin whisp of something white drifting by that wall of brush.

'What the tarnal is that?' Lomas whispered.

'Smoke,' Ellington said triumphantly, grinning across at Claggett. 'And like they say, where there's smoke there's just bound to be fire.'

7

Blood Moon

Dunbar remained still watching the canyon.

The evening sounds came to him familiarly — the mechanical clank of the ore-crusher where Stolbeck was still at work . . . the braying of the mules indicating they were getting hungry . . . the distant clatter of pots and pans from the house as Amy fixed supper.

Everything appeared the same as the last time he looked — or was it? Dunbar slowly realized that things were almost the same, which was a very different thing.

A tinhorn might ignore such a sensation but a pro like himself had to rely on his senses and so took his feelings seriously.

He stood by the smokehouse in the

crimson wash of the dying daylight. His gaze raked the canyon rim, left, right, then left again. Nothing. The brush was still and nothing stirred until a dusty giant tumbleweed rolled slowly down the cliff slope and vanished lazily from sight.

Ever since his instincts had started acting up, Dunbar had been up to the rim twice, each time without sighting anything. He was tempted to go up again now while there was still light, but decided against it. He reminded himself that a man's sixth sense could prove notoriously unreliable at times.

The crimson wash of sundown was dying as he finally quit the shed and headed off to a check on the mules. The animals greeted him with a great chorus of braying and he was grinning as he fed them hay, thinking how much the big brown critter with one eye reminded him of the governor of Texas.

He was relaxed by the time he'd finished the chore and returned to the house. He paused to sniff the cooking aromas drifting down the walkway before entering his room.

He saw the flowers right off. They had been placed in a cracked crockery vase upon the bureau by the window. They were wild desert flowers and he knew instantly that she had picked them for him.

For a time he sat on the edge of his bunk and gazed around. The room was simple and sparsely furnished. He'd stayed in plush hotels from New Orleans to San Francisco in his time, yet this ten-by-ten outshone them all. How come? Because Amy Stolbeck kept it neat and put flowers in the vase, that was how come.

Lost in thought he was suddenly aware of a light footfall behind causing him to swivel with right hand wrapped around gunbutt.

Amy stood framed in the doorway, looking startled.

'Why, Shell!' she cried. 'What's the matter?'

He glanced down at the gun, put it

away in an instant. 'Sorry, Amy. I guess I'm a little jumpy tonight.'

She nodded understandingly. 'Is that the reason you went up on the rim twice?'

He smiled wryly. 'You don't miss much, do you? By the way, thanks for the flowers.'

'They're white cacanillas.'

'They are? Reckon I've never been much on flowers.'

She studied him thoughtfully for a moment. 'You're still tense, Shell.'

Realizing he'd been fidgeting with his belt buckle, Dunbar folded his arms. 'Yeah, damned if I know why.'

'I believe I know.'

'You do?'

'I think you miss your regular work and you're fretting to get back to it.'

'Maybe. But somehow I don't think that's it.'

He went to the window to gaze over the canyon again. Amy went out on to the gallery where she stood at the top of the steps. He studied her in silence.

He would give a lot to know what was going on behind those sky-blue eyes right now. He sensed she might be attracted to him, yet was aware that he could easily be misreading simple friendliness.

There was no telling for sure. Amy Stolbeck was a lovely enigma with a will of her own, deep as a river.

He finally set a cigarillo alight and quit the room to join the girl on the gallery. They stood together watching the first diamond-point stars blink into life in the vast arch of the sky. He leaned against an upright, dividing his attention between the woman and the length of the darkening canyon rim. The stogie was relaxing him now and he felt good.

At length Amy turned to face him. 'So, when will you be leaving us, Shell?'

'Soon, I guess . . . ' He sounded vague.

'To return to bounty hunting, of course?'

'It's what I know.'

'You're the first bounty hunter I ever met.'

He smiled. 'Well, I guess that proves you've led a respectable life.'

She didn't return his smile. 'I've had some experience with lawmen, though, unpleasant in the main.'

'Yeah?'

'Oh, I've never been in trouble with the law, but I have seen the way some operate. I must admit I was far from impressed.'

He shrugged. 'Well, you know how things can be, Amy. There's good and bad in all walks of life. Maybe you just struck the bad.'

'They were blind and intractible, Shell,' she said with feeling. 'Men who didn't think for themselves but allowed a pile of dusty law books do their thinking and deciding for them. So, tell me, are you a machine man also?'

Feeling vaguely uneasy, Shell puffed on his Cuban to set up a smokescreen. The truth was he'd been accused of that very shortcoming more than once.

It had been said of him that the Revised Statutes of Texas, 1885, was Shell Dunbar's bible. He had been labelled as seeing matters of guilt or innocence in black and white only — lawful or unlawful. And never the twain should meet, other than in a courtroom or over gunsights.

He knew no other way. But how did you make a young woman understand that? You couldn't. So you changed the subject.

'Time's slipping by, Amy. You want I should go fetch your father for supper?'

She studied at him as though aware he was being evasive. But she nodded. 'Yes, do that. It will be ready by the time you get back.'

As he stepped by her, he lightly touched her arm. He didn't kiss her, made no attempt to do so, yet sensed she would not have resisted. He smiled, was startled when she spoke softly;

'I like you, Shell Dunbar.'

'Why . . . why, I'm real glad to hear that, Amy.'

'But the word is 'like',' she said firmly, turning away. 'Please don't get that confused with anything else.'

He stood staring after her as she went down the walkway, nodded slowly to himself. 'Were you reminding *me* not to get serious — or yourself, pretty woman?' he murmured, then turned away and headed for the mine.

He'd not covered half the distance when he spotted the mule that resembled the governor. While the other animals were still chomping on their feed 'Gov' stood in a corner of the corral with ears sticking straight up, mismatched eyes focused upon the cliff above the canyon's east rim.

Gazing in that direction Dunbar thought he caught a stir of movement in the brush that might have been caused by a breeze, except there was no breeze. He sensed that whatever it was he'd seen had appeared solid . . . could even have been a man.

Without pause — heart beating quicker — he kept on to the mine, was cool and unruffled as usual as he told Stolbeck to report to the washhouse and kitchen in that order.

But underneath he was tense. Whatever he'd half-seen had set alarm bells clanging. Something or somebody was up there; he was sure of it. It was his job to find out what it was without alarming the Stolbecks.

Returning to the house with Rooney he insisted he'd lost his appetite and meant to take a stroll to retrieve it. Rooney seemed indifferent but Amy showed concern as he made for the door.

'You take care and don't go too far, Shell,' she cautioned.

'Tush! Leave the man be, child,' Rooney grumbled. 'He's old enough to look out for himself.'

The bounty man's instincts seemed to warn him that he might be called upon to to prove this before this Seven Sisters night was much older.

★ ★ ★

Beneath the lopsided moon the desert landscape gave up its scents of sage and wild flowers, all prospering in this brief season now before summer's full heat burnt them back into the dust.

The moon silvered the coiling wraiths of fog raised by the nightwind and invested them with a ghostly sheen.

From Dunbar's point of view the moon had timed things just right, holding back its arrival long enough for him to make it up the canyon wall in the last of the darkness. Now it spilled its cold metallic light for him as he lay lizard-like in a cactus shadow, eyes scanning the nocturnal landscape.

Everything he saw might well have been an enemy; each clump or boulder a possible heller with a gun until proven otherwise.

Uneventful minutes dragged by. He moved on, wriggling belly-flat through soft sand. He held the rifle in his right hand and packed two Colts in his shell belt, with an ammunition belt slung across his chest. There was some risk of the weapons brushing rock and making a noise but this was outweighed by the greater risk of being caught under-armed if trouble erupted.

He found the single footprint a short time later between a barrel cactus and the bleached skull of some long-dead animal. It was barely distinguishable as a print, for the nightwind was already filling the indentation with sand. But it was enough. He tightened his grip on the rifle and slipped into a crouch to follow the sign.

He was about to come as close to sudden death as he'd ever done.

It happened as he inched his way around that first clump of twisted black rock that was the legacy of an ancient lava spill. He gave the formation a cursory glance as he approached but was more concerned with the prints before him which seemed to be leading directly to a deep natural saucer in the earth on the near side of the malpai ridge.

There was no need for him to glance

up as he wriggled by the rock base, yet had he done so he would have sighted the astonished, square jawed mug of Moe Archer gaping down on him.

Archer had been keeping watch from the lookout point ever since sundown when he'd relieved Lomas. During that time, Lomas and Ellington had been resting up a short distance away in the saucer where the outlaws had made their camp, leaving Claggett to take off on another precautionary survey of the canyon. During the afternoon all four had combed the canyon, and while Ellington, Lomas and Archer had been eager to get on with the business at hand they'd nonetheless felt obliged to respect Claggett's caution.

The leader wanted no mistakes, meant to wait until Dunbar was in close range and impossible to miss.

Dunbar was close to that exact distance which separated him from Archer at that very moment.

But Dunbar had materialized so swiftly it took Archer a moment to recover from the shock when he saw him.

The realization that Dunbar had managed to quit the canyon unseen then arrived so close to their camp was a chilling reminder of the breed of man they were up against.

But a bullet brings every man down to the same size, Archer reminded himself and instantly lifted rifle to shoulder. The ivory bead of the rifle steadied upon Dunbar's broad chest and the killer was raising the hindsight to notch the foresight when Lomas's voice sounded from behind.

'Hey, Archer, you want some chow?'

It was just a whisper. But to Dunbar it sounded more like a shout that galvanized him into action, rolling and kicking for deep cover a split second before Archer squeezed trigger.

The moment Archer fired he knew he'd missed.

Furiously jacking a fresh shell into the chamber, he arced his gunsights in a desperate search pattern. But Dunbar was blasting even as he retreated and the outlaw howled and dropped flat when a rifle thundered and the bounty hunter's bullet whipped past his face so close he felt the hot breath of its passage.

Dunbar had fired from the hip, missed, yet not by much. So close in fact it galvanised Dunbar into a desperate dive that carried him behind a clump of twisted malpai.

Bobbing up, Dunbar glimpsed dark figures rushing towards a bunch of tethered horses in a draw close by. Instantly he blasted off a shot that raked across Archer's back. The man staggered but didn't fall, recovering to whirl and touch off a shot that dusted Dunbar's face with powdered rock as it ricocheted.

By the time he'd risen warily the outlaws were figures circling on horse-back, while Archer appeared to have vanished.

He sprang from cover to make for a high crest thirty feet distant. He was lightning fast and needed to be. As he gained the high ground the riders were circling at maybe fifty yards distant, barely visible in the gloom, but vulnerable, he hoped.

He pressed rifle butt against cheek and jerked trigger.

It was a good shot but not quite good enough.

The rifle thundered again and the lead rider was almost unseated when the bullet nicked his horse's neck, causing it to rear wildly before it recovered and rushed on.

The outlaws were fanning out now and had almost crested the malpai ridge. This seemed too far for a stopping shot but Dunbar knew he had to try.

He dropped belly flat and rested the barrel across a stunted greasewood. A rider was bearing in to the right and he thought he glimpsed Archer. He took aim and squeezed the trigger gently. For a moment horse and rider were obscured by gunsmoke. When it cleared he saw the rider tumbling end over end in a great ball of powdery dust.

When the man stopped rolling he never moved again.

There was no quarter asked or given in the battle that raged at the Overman after Shell made it back safely in the wake of one man's violent death.

The first hour was uncertain with the outlaws mounting swift attacks on horseback, sweeping in shooting then breaking up to regroup when harassed by the defence guns.

At the end of that hour Shell realized the situation appeared grim, despite the good work done by Rooney with his big Fifty, with Amy reloading for them both.

There was no thought of compromise and towards dawn Claggett opened up a furious cover fire to keep Dunbar tied down then sent Lomas and Ellington in.

The close clash of arms that resulted was fierce and relentless, and well before Claggett was forced to pull back to regroup Shell sensed that this could only end one way. The enemy had the numbers and when they nailed him as they must, it would be all over.

Better to deal while he was still alive and knew how to deal, he decided.

Claggett proved amenable, displaying both his confidence and his courage by coming in alone after the defenders suggested peace talks.

These proved long and lengthy and did nothing to favour the defenders. In the end, the best a tight-lipped Dunbar could secure was the promise of safe passage out for himself and the family, leaving the mine and the gold to the enemy. The victors 'generously' conceded the losers time to wind things up here before getting gone, but rejected their request for a week to do it. Three days, was Claggett's top offer, and they knew he meant it.

8

Close Quarters Kill

The mule that resembled the governor of Texas was not to be found in the brushy draws of the canyon, nor anywhere in the cool recesses of the mine itself. With these possibilities eliminated that left but one conclusion. The critter had chewed its way through the gate rope of the corral overnight and wandered off into the desert.

'He'll come back,' predicted Dunbar, standing by the stables with Stolbeck. 'There's next to no feed to be had up there and no water for miles.'

'You don't understand that there critter, mister,' Stolbeck muttered. 'He's so cross-grained stubborn he wouldn't back up and admit he'd made a mistake even if he died for it. Nope, I'll just have to go find him.'

'Are you loco? They're out there someplace watching our every move. In truth I'm surprised the scum haven't moved in on us before we're through closing down.'

'All the more reason for me to track Sherman down before he comes to any harm.'

They argued until Shell realized the other was dead serious; nothing would dissuade him from going after the animal. It was then he faced the inevitable. If anybody must go search, then it would be him.

Rooney looked emotional when told. 'You mean you'd do that for me, mister? Glory be, but I ain't sure I deserve a friend as fine as that.'

'You don't.' Shell was blunt and honest. 'But if you want to know the truth, mister, I'm doing this more for myself than you. I've known for some time I'd have to go take a scout around before we even think about moving out. Sure, we got a deal, but that's like having a deal with the devil. We can't sit about forever waiting to see if they'll attack, so this is as good a time as any to reconnoitre.'

'I sure won't forget this, mister.'

'Just so long as you don't forget you'll be in charge here while I'm gone. Don't even think of doing any packing up yourself, just sit with your rifle and keep sharp. Now saddle one of these critters for me while I go fetch my canteen.'

'A brave man through and through, Jessie,' Rooney confided to the mule he selected. 'You know, it just could be that Amy is right about him. Mebbe I should trust him after all . . . '

The mule bared yellow teeth. She was even more distrustful of strangers than Rooney, which was going some.

★   ★   ★

The horsefly saved Dunbar's life. If it hadn't bitten the mule's hindquarters just as Dunbar was closing in on his quarry at the end of a two-hour search, the mule would not have pig-rooted and almost thrown the rider. It took some time to bring the critter under control, and it was inside that time that Dunbar spotted the rope stretched tightly across the trail ahead at just the right height to cause the animal to trip.

The enemy had set a trap!

His head snapped up and he glimpsed a blur of movement in the brush close by and ducked instinctively a moment before the rifle roared and something zipped by close and slammed into the mule's chest, killing it instantly.

Kicking free, Shell landed on his feet, staggered, righted himself with the aid of the rifle then plunged wildly for cover as bullets whipped about his pumping legs. He reached a downward slope and went tumbling headlong down it and could hear the killers shouting and cursing above their gunblasts.

Halfway down the slope he threaded his way off through a scatter of sizeable boulders. He covered a mile before being forced to dive headlong into a crevice and take stock, every sense clamouring.

The shooting had ceased but the acrid stink of gunsmoke drifting down warned that danger was very close. Twisting his head this way and that, he quickly decided he was relatively safe in this crevice even though there was no detectable way out without revealing himself.

He went low as a heavy slug smashed into the protecting rocks and the roar of the rifle sounded chillingly close, the echoes beating far across the canyon.

'You're done for, hot-shot!' a big voice bawled. 'No way out — so show yourself and get it over quick!'

The killers hadn't wasted any time getting into position, he could tell. He set his rifle aside and set about gathering rocks to build a sturdy low breastworks, the sweat stinging his eyes and catching in his throat as he worked at furious pace. Several times rifles crashed close by, and he knew they would surely kill him if they staged a concerted rush. But that plainly was a sizeable 'if'. They'd be forced to expose themselves to get to him and would surely pay for that with blood.

At last he was able to stretch out and gather his breath. He had left some chinks in his breastworks for visibility. He could see the entire northern wall of the canyon from a certain angle, and occasionally glimpsed movement amongst the rocks some fifty to sixty feet distant. Assessing his situation calmly he concluded there should be little danger from the flanks or the rear; the only way they might reach him would be frontally.

He popped a pebble into his mouth and sucked on it to assuage his thirst. Eventually the sun drenched the canyon in a flood of fire. High above, a lone buzzard glided on lazy wings. Waiting.

★　★　★

The desert was still.

The morning wind had played out after noon and nothing stirred. The dead mule lay on its back, bloated like a water-filled goatskin with legs thrust upwards like sticks. In the intense heat the carcass had begun to stink, the smell hanging in the sullen air like the essence of death and corruption.

Claggett had fashioned a sunbreak from his slicker and sticks, yet sprawled full length in the rocks on the northern rim of the canyon the shade merely covered head and torso, leaving his legs exposed and burning under the sun.

Some thirty feet off to his right the slim-hipped Ellington lay belly flat and propped up on his elbows as he squinted through a vee formed by two rocks. The killer was unprotected apart from his hat yet seemingly not bothered by the heat.

Claggett studied his gun segundo enviously, wondering if this sort of life was really only for men as young and tough as Ellington.

Due to his wounded arm, Lomas had been allowed to take up a position beneath a heavy rock overhang well back from the other two, but where he would still be close should Dunbar make a break for it. Claggett figured that break would have to come soon. Dunbar must be drying out like a cork leg down there without a drop to drink.

Archer stared up at the pitiless sky and instantly regretted it. The brilliant light seemed to bore into his skull. He blinked and sighted a black speck against the intense brightness of the sky. It was a zopilote, the small turkey-buzzard. It was most likely a scout, he figured, hunting for food for the flock. The scent of the dead mule had likely drawn the devil bird, but Archer knew it would have shown up sooner or later even without the scent. Looking for him. Buzzards knew when someone was about to die ahead of time. Nobody understood how they did it — but they always knew.

★   ★   ★

Each time they heard a shot, Amy Stolbeck would count off another bead of her rosary.

The set of beads was well worn, though not by her fingers. Her mother had been devoutly religious but Amy only ever resorted to prayer when unhappy or racked by fear, as now.

Yet her fears were not for herself but for Shell Dunbar. She'd realized immediately that the shooting they'd heard earlier indicated Shell had found trouble quickly, despite her father's lame reassurances to the contrary. He'd tried to convince her that the shooting merely indicated Dunbar was likely only driving the coyotes away.

Amy had been against Shell leaving the canyon and had tried to dissuade him. But in the end it had come down to a choice between either Dunbar or Rooney going after the mule and Dunbar had volunteered. She stared across the front room at her rifle-toting father now with something like hate in her eyes.

'Goldurn, don't stare at me like that, girl,' Rooney objected. 'What was I supposed to do? Just let old Sherman die of thirst out there and not lift a finger?'

'They'll kill him,' she stated flatly. 'Then they'll come for us.'

Rooney slapped the worn, polished stock of his Big Fifty and puffed out his chest. 'Then they'll regret that till their dyin' day,' he predicted. 'Every murderous one of them. Yes, sir, they'll find that the blood of the fightin' dukes still runs strong in Rooney Stolbeck if they force me into a corner . . . yes sir, you can bet on that!'

Amy dropped her gaze to her beads. She couldn't look at her father any longer.

★   ★   ★

A horse galloped down that nameless canyon, a pure white stallion with streaming tail and mane, the flashing hoofs making no sound upon the hard, sun-whitened rocks.

Dunbar's red-rimmed eyes followed the beautiful beast in wonderment, then

150

saw it changing shape . . . until it was transformed into some amorphous creature of fable, then a ghost, and finally metamorphized into nothing more substantial than a drifting tatter of gunsmoke dissolving slowly away through the shadows.

His head came down to rest on his arms.

Hallucinations.

He'd suffered them once before in the Arizonan desert when he ran out of water on the trail of Black Bob Durell.

Pure life-saving luck had led him to an old desert rat's camp near the spring, that day. The oldster had told him that when you started seeing things you were just a short step from going out of your mind altogether. 'When the mind finally goes, it cracks like a whip, mister!' the old-timer had said, snapping his fingers to illustrate. 'Like that!'

Shell refused to believe a man could lose his senses that suddenly, yet knew he was in perilously bad shape. Endless hours in the Seven Sisters hellhole without a drop of water and the sun slamming down into his rock hole had sapped his strength and put putty in his muscles where sinews and bone used to be.

The terrain across from his retreat no longer resembled a canyon slope dotted with large boulders and clumps of sage. It was a blurred tan wall that swam in his vision even now after the heat haze was gone.

He stretched his lips in a mirthless grin. These hardcases knew their business. Novice hardcases would have most likely attempted to shoehorn him out of his safe-hole, and likely died. But Claggett was a pro who'd sat back and waited for sun and thirst to do their brutal work before moving in.

And the punishment was working. That yellow sun now sinking towards the rim of the world . . . another hour of that and he would be all through.

Dunbar slammed the heel of his hand against his temple, forcing himself to think clearly for maybe the last time.

One hour left?

That hour would bring darkness and they would come slinking like coyotes to finish off a hamstrung beast. They would come silently and stealthily and slaughter him with their guns and by then he might not even know he was being killed.

He stared upwards. Sunset hurled flaming colours across the big sky, beginning to fade a little now, narrowing down swiftly to one final streak of crimson. He would die, and all that was left for him was to decide how.

Living a dangerous life, he'd never been afraid of death, and it puzzled him why he was so inclined to cling to life so fiercely now death appeared inevitable.

Next moment he had his answer. Amy. It was a hard thing, he decided, to roam the earth for twenty-five years before finding love, then die while it was still fresh and new. And he wondered if there was any truth in the old adage — better to have loved and lost than never to have loved at all.

Crash!

The shot startled him, and he realized they were getting ready. The shadows were deepening and they were eager to get it done. After a minute he rose to his knees and forced his vision to function clearly again by a sheer act of will. He hefted the Winchester and it was like embracing an old companion. It was for him to decide how he would go — die like a rat in a hole or stand and go out with some style.

No choice at all, really.

He would be satisfied if he just took one with him, Ellington for preference.

Abruptly he rose with the rifle and blasted at a vague shape. As the report died away he heard the big man's belly laugh drift down.

'He's shootin' at shadows now, boys!' Claggett gloated. 'Hey, Dunbar, why don't you come share this ice-cold spring water we got here? Plenty to spare and you're more than welcome!'

'Buckets of it!' Ellington yelled, and slammed a shot into his barricade.

Shell glanced at the sky. Sunset was reduced to just one slender pink bar now. He told himself that when the bar disappeared he would step out and die fighting. But, how come it was so quiet of a sudden. What were they doing now?

★ ★ ★

Leaning against the natural barricade of the rock slope, Lomas flexed the arm that had been giving him hell and tried to convince himself the pain would vanish after he'd emptied his rifle into Dunbar's lousy carcass.

Close by, Ellington methodically loaded the magazine of his Winchester repeater from his shell belt while Claggett lifted the cap from the metal canteen and drank deep. The big man was facing Lomas who suddenly saw his eyes, above the canteen, snap wide in surprise.

Whirling, Colt .45 in hand, Lomas immediately saw what had caught

155

Luke's attention.

Coming slowly across towards them over the yellow sand flats from the trackless south, was a rider.

'What the blue hell — ?' Ellington breathed. 'Who in Hades is this, Luke?'

'Am I supposed to know every damn thing?' Claggett barked, working the action of his big rifle. 'But one thing I see is that he ain't nobody we know, and we sure as shootin' don't want no strangers hornin' in on this turkey-shoot!'

With those words he blasted a shot into the sky and the distant rider drew rein.

'Git!' Claggett roared, accompanying the order with a violent gesture.

'What's goin' on?' came the response.

'None of your nevermind!'

'Who's down that there canyon?' the stranger wanted to know.

'Judas Priest, Luke!' Ellington rasped, 'this one is beggin' for it!'

Claggett cut his eyes down slope and caught a flicker of movement from Dunbar's position. For a moment the big man stood locked motionless, then made a sudden gesture. 'Give him what he craves, then.'

Ellington and Lomas needed no prompting. Yet as their rifles swung up, the rider on the black horse raised a rifle one-handed, triggered once and sent Lomas to ground with a bullet in the kneecap, howling.

The cry of agony penetrated Dunbar's brain like a knife, jerking him back from the shadowy border ground of hallucination, stripping some of the glaze from his eyes. The action was below his line of vision yet he had a glimpse of an outlaw pointing his rifle westwards. Lomas's howls of agony drowned out whatever they were yelling now.

Rooney?

Shell found it hard to believe the old-timer would have come out looking for him. But if not Stolbeck, then who? Somebody with a good gun eye by the sound of all that yelling and shooting up there — but surely whoever it was had to be somebody who might use some back-up?

He clambered groggily from his rocky niche, flexed arms and legs, made unsteadily for the canyon floor.

A hundred yards upslope from the earthern mound where Claggett and Ellington had sheltered to return the stranger's fire, Lomas was the only one to witness Shell's appearance. With one hand clutching his shattered knee and the other on the rifle, Lomas twisted his head to alert his henchmen but his voice was drowned out by gun-song.

Lomas clenched his teeth. Leg or no leg, he would have to deal with Dunbar himself.

Upon gaining the canyon floor without getting shot to doll rags, Shell Dunbar had found renewed strength. He now began clambering up towards the outlaws' positions. His legs remained rubbery but his blood was pumping strongly now and his vision was clearing by the moment.

He was halfway up the slope when

Lomas's head and shoulders showed above the rim through a tangle of yellow grass above.

Instantly Shell jerked trigger — and Lomas scored none out of two shots when Dunbar threw himself sideways, rolled violently, kicked up into a kneeling position with the still smoking rifle extended before him. His left hand jacked a stream of hot spent shells from the chamber while the right kept working the trigger.

His aim was shaky but sheer firepower compensated. Three shots missed the crippled Lomas before one caught him in the belly. Instantly another bullet drilled his rotten heart and he snapped erect, hugging himself as though suddenly cold. The next two shots that thudded home sent the badman skittering backwards to stumble over Jimmy Ellington's outstretched legs, flattening the hardcase with his dead weight when he crashed atop him.

Shell legged it faster to the crest and only then sighted the stranger. He had just a momentary glimpse of head and shoulders but it was enough to strike a chord of memory and identify the man as friendly. And, severely affected by heat and deprivation as he was, he desperately welcomed any friend he could get right now as he headed for the west end of the canyon.

9

Colt Justice

Clint Buckner sloshed another generous jolt of rye whiskey into the coffee Amy had brewed for him.

'Some things change but I doubt Texan hospitality ever does, eh, Rooney?' he drawled. Then sobering as he looked across the table at the girl, 'Nor Texas beauty, Amy love.' He raised his mug. 'To Texas hospitality and Texas beauty, may neither ever disappear from this ugly old world!'

It was after midnight. There had been no sign of Claggett and Ellington since the pair launched their attack following the arrival of Dunbar and Buckner, which the defenders had successfully beaten off. The shades were now tightly drawn and the trio were taking it in turns to stand watch from the darkened gallery.

It came time for Rooney to relieve Shell, and Dunbar was glad to see him. Even after the big meal Amy had whipped up, plus all the water he could take in, he was still far from feeling chipper.

Taking a seat in a corner with a cigarillo between his teeth, he watched Amy and Buckner together and listened to them talk.

They were sweethearts of long standing. Dunbar had learned this early and had picked up on a lot more since.

Buckner was the son of a United States senator from Clantonville County, East Texas. The Buckners had owned the cattle ranch adjoining the Stolbecks which vastly oustripped them in both size and prosperity. Amy and Buckner had attended school together, had finally fallen in love and had begun to make wedding plans.

Then Rooney became involved in his high-stake card game and the Stolbecks were ruined overnight.

Dunbar sensed clearly that Amy's clan agreed that the daughter of a bankrupt was hardly a fitting wife for the son of a senator.

As a result the proud Stolbecks had loaded what was left in a buckboard and pushed westwards in search of a fortune, and Rooney had duly paid off his creditors. Amy and Clint still intended to wed, and meanwhile Buckner visited them from time to time in the Seven Sisters.

Shell drew thoughtfully on his smoke. He understood now what Rooney had meant when he'd warned him his suit was hopeless, while Buckner's sudden arrival in the middle of the battle seemed to explain why he had only made a certain amount of progress with Amy and no more.

Yet he puzzled why they hadn't told him about Buckner in the first place. Buckner and Amy were lovers; it happened every day. It would have been easy enough for Amy to simply tell him there was somebody else.

Why hadn't she done so?

But time would heal it all . . . maybe. He could live with this, but what about the other thing?

He forced himself to examine that seemingly unworthy suspicion he'd nursed all along that Buckner didn't seem to sit right — to his eyes, that was.

Yet he reminded himself that the man was a senator's son. He had proven himself a man in coming out here at such a dangerous time, and had all the credentials of a gentleman.

Dunbar was jealous. He grimaced at the thought, wanted to think he was above that. But what man knew his own strengths and weaknesses until they had been put to the test?

Amy and Clint quit talking when he rose and made for the door. 'Where are you going, Shell?' Amy asked worriedly.

'Guess I'll go take another look around. Can't be too careful.'

'With you,' Clint said. He rose swiftly, kissed the top of Amy's head then crossed the room to get his rifle with his lithe athletic step. 'Who knows? We could get lucky and bag some big game.'

'Really, Clint,' Amy chided. 'You shouldn't talk that way. After all, they're human beings.'

'Only just . . . mebbe,' Buckner grinned, making for the door. 'Right, Dunbar?'

Shell just shrugged and scooped up his rifle. 'Meet you out front,' he murmured, and went out.

He seemed clearer in the head and fully revived by the time he stood gazing out over the moonwashed canyon a short spell later. The night now appeared quiet under a silver moon but there was only one way of being sure how things really were. He'd have to take a patrol.

When Buckner emerged they headed off into the moonlight with Rooney covering them from the porch with the Big Henry.

Reaching a patch of deep shadow Dunbar paused to light up. He realized

Buckner was studying him intently, when he said, 'You're in love with my girl, aren't you, Shell?'

'What kind of question is that?'

'You're not going to deny it, are you?'

He took a deep breath. Buckner was an impressive man, handsome, big-shouldered and supremely self-assured. He also had the right background and qualifications to complete the picture of the perfect suitor for any woman of quality.

'OK,' he said eventually, 'I'm fond of her . . . if that's important.'

Buckner studied him a moment longer; there was no telling what he might be thinking, whether he was angry, jealous, or simply didn't care. He was a man very hard to read. At last he shrugged and moved off across the house yard with Shell following.

'All right, down to business. Tell me, Shell, what would you do if you were big Claggett right now?'

They paused in the shadow of the ore-crusher. Shell fingered his hat back as he gazed around. 'Reckon I'd quit altogether and head off.'

'Do you see him as the quitting kind?'

'He's shown no sign of it. But I've a hunch I know what makes Claggett tick. His strength and weaknesses are one and the same thing.'

'Huh?'

'Pride. I've seen this too often in outlaws I've dealt with not to recognize it. He's never forgotten I bested him in San Paulo, and he's bragged to everyone he'll take us both and the gold, and he's got to live up to that boast.'

Buckner appeared thoughtful. 'You know a lot about outlaws, I guess?'

'It's my business to know.'

'Uh-huh, OK. So, let's take a look at this situation. If we agree that scum bunch won't quit, I guess it stands to reason that they would be watching us?'

'I would be if I was in their boots.'

'Claggett's lost men, scored some dinero, but he's still hungry for more,' Clint murmured, thinking out loud.

'Maybe by now he's getting desperate on account he feels he's just got to win big here.'

'So?'

He was checking this man out, needed to know what he was made of should things come to a showdown.

'So . . . maybe we can get him to come to us instead of trying to flush him out? It's plain if we don't nail him by first light we'll have to go after him.'

'Night offers the best odds . . . and it's just them or us now,' Dunbar said.

'Uh-huh, them or us, I like that.' Buckner's big smile suddenly flashed. 'Maybe it's not up to me to make suggestions to a big-time bounty man like you, Shell, but I'd like to try something to get them to come to us. You want to hear?'

'Fire away.'

'I like a man with an open mind,' Clint Buckner declared. Then pausing to relight his cigar, he began to talk fast.

★ ★ ★

It was a half-hour later when the faint sounds of argument drifted up to the killers sprawled out side by side upon the canyon rim.

Stirring sharply, Claggett and Ellington peered down.

They quickly realized the voices were coming from the stables near the draw which ran past the corral. In the darkness, the outlaws had heard voices and movement below some time earlier, followed some time later by the clink of bottle against glass.

Now the voices grew louder until they were suddenly swallowed by the muffled boom of a shot.

In the silence that followed, Rooney Stolbeck and the girl appeared upon the gallery of the house to peer towards the stables. Next moment, the stable doors burst open and Shell Dunbar reeled out into the dim moonlight clutching a six-gun in his fist. He blasted a shot through the doorway, then staggered away, heading for the draw.

Moments later the stranger emerged from the stables brandishing a rifle and shouting curses. Dunbar whirled to blast a shot in the man's direction, then continued on for the draw again. The stranger dropped into a crouch and sent a slug whistling after him. Amy Stolbeck screamed as Dunbar staggered and the stranger started after him, bawling, 'You double-crossing Judas, Dunbar!'

Next moment the startled watchers saw Dunbar tumble down the slope of the draw then struggle to his knees, still clutching his Colt.

The moment the other man reached the rim of the draw, both men triggered. The stranger yelled and fell. As he rolled downslope towards Dunbar, the bounty man fired at him at point blank range.

He kicked the motionless body before starting back upslope. The couple on the gallery started for the steps but propped when Dunbar suddenly staggered, clutched at his chest, took one step back, another forward, then fell.

Claggett and Ellington watched in astonishment as Stolbeck rushed to Dunbar's side and the girl began to shriek, 'He's dead! Oh, he's dead.'

The outlaws traded a confounded glance then switched back to the scene below. By this the girl had vanished inside — and neither sprawled figure had moved an inch.

'Do you smell a rat, Claggett?'

'Dunno. What do you reckon?'

'Must really be dead . . . I guess.'

'What if they're fakin'?'

Claggett rubbed his black beard. Their plan had been to wait and watch until around three o'clock when the defenders' vigilance might be expected to be at its poorest, when they would strike hard and fast. Having lost both Lomas and Archer with little gain they needed to come out on top here. But this latest incident left them in two minds. Was what they were seeing a bloody falling out in the enemy camp — or some kind of trick?

Time ticked by. No sound from the

house. The 'dead' men didn't stir. Another long stillness, then Ellington hissed, 'What do you figure?'

'I-I reckon we gotta get down there. If we circle the house and come on to the draw with a clear line of fire, we can fill those two with lead — just to make double sure they're as dead as they look now. What do you say?'

Ellington laughed, the deep confident sound of a man who believed in himself and his gun above all else. 'I say let's get to it.'

★　★　★

They came stalking down the west flank of the house with the stealth of marauding coyotes, darting from cover to cover, the fading moonlight shimmering on the weapons they had in their hands. They made no sound, pausing every few yards to glance at the house and then at the draw. The girl had stopped weeping. The building lay in darkness.

As far as they could see the dark figures in the draw hadn't moved.

They reached the tack room without incident. It was the final cover before the draw. The open space which stretched before them was totally innocent of life or movement, which was a mite reassuring if not completely so. So they waited a spell longer while an uncaring moon looked down.

Suddenly there was no point in tarrying any longer, and Luke breathed, 'Now!' and they stepped into the open side by side.

Within the darkened house, crouching by the side window which was opened just far enough to accommodate the barrel of the Henry Big Fifty, little Rooney Stolbeck prayed for a steady hand and keen eye.

The outlaws ghosted into his line of vision. They had drawn within range in moments and the lethal Ellington was raising his rifle to his shoulder now.

'Now, Pa!' Amy hissed and, tensing his body, Rooney breathed in and gently stroked trigger.

The crash of the big weapon sounded insanely loud in the stillness, and as the thick smoke cleared, Jimmy Ellington was to be seen falling to his knees and threshing violently as though grappling with an invisible enemy. But Claggett was unhurt and rushed towards the house with a terrible roar, fired blindly, not sighting the two figures leaping to their feet in the draw until they came charging towards him behind blazing guns.

Somehow the badly wounded Ellington managed to raise his gun and was triggering as Claggett whirled and ran. Storming guns argued violently back and forth as Buckner and Dunbar came charging in at a weaving, crouching run moments before Ellington the killer was reefed to his feet by the terrible impact of the volley that caught him squarely in the chest and he performed a hideous dance of death before pitching down face forwards in the dust.

Claggett somehow made it all the

way before Buckner's rifle slammed a
.32 slug through his side. He somer-
saulted, crashed headlong into the wall
of the shack, then twisted ashen-faced
to fire back. But Dunbar had surged
well ahead of Buckner by this and was
fanning Colt hammer from waist level
with the first bullet catching Claggett's
shoulder and the next slamming him
back against the wall yet again.

An animal sound escaped the killer's
throat. Streaming blood, his body one
searing flame of agony, he glared at the
threatening figures through a red mist
— and came apart.

'Don't kill me! In God's name
— don't!'

'Keep praying, you bastard!' Buckner
snarled, and levelled his rifle.

'Leave him go!' Shell yelled. 'He's all
through!'

Too late. Clint Buckner's Winchester
crashed and the final bullet smashed
home between Claggett's bulging eyes.

10

The Final Guns

The wind blew dust across the new graves that would soon become part of the desert again. Rooney Stolbeck and Shell Dunbar stood with their heads uncovered. Clint Buckner was just a short distance away, leaning on a shovel. He wore his hat and puffed on a cigar. It was early morning and the heat had yet to warm the dust blowing across the Seven Sisters.

Rooney rubbed his nose and looked at Shell.

'Do you know any words, mister?'

Dunbar cleared his throat and quoted something remembered from the dark day his father was laid to rest.

'He shall take them away as with the whirlwind, both living, and in his wrath. The righteous shall rejoice when he seeth the vengeance; he shall wash his feet in the blood of the wicked. So men shall say, 'Verily, there is reward for the righteous; verily he is a God that judgeth in the earth'.'

'Amen,' said Rooney solemnly. And that desert wind did blow.

★   ★   ★

Clint's voice carried clearly out to the gallery where Shell sat behind the screen of vines, cleaning his rifle.

' . . . So I suggested to Dad that he should retire before next election to give me the chance to fill his place and get to know the electors. He seemed to think it a good idea, though of course he felt obliged to point out that a few things needed clearing up before I could run for office.' A pause, then he summarized in a more sober tone, 'Of course these things cost money . . . '

'You know I'd like to help, boy,' Rooney stated. 'I only wish I was in a position to do so, but — '

Dunbar didn't hear any more as he got to his feet and went down the steps. It was high noon in the Seven Sisters and the morning wind had fallen away until now the day was still as the tomb. Across in the corral the mules stood beneath their brushwood ramada, hip-shot and twitching flies. The outlaws' mounts were yarded with Buckner's stallion in the adjoining corral where Amy was feeding them hay from her hand.

His expression pensive, Shell played his gaze around the rim. It seemed incredibly quiet and peaceful in the wake of the chaos of recent days.

He frowned unconsciously as he turned to stare across at the tack room where Claggett had died. He'd censured Buckner for killing Claggett when the man was helpless, though hardly severely. Men did things in the heat of battle they would not normally do, he well knew. He only wished Buckner hadn't looked so damn excited when he pulled trigger that last time.

The sun struck like a hammer blow

as he went down the steps and headed for the stables. Sighting him, Amy fed the last of the hay to the stallion then strolled across to intercept him as he approached the stable doors.

'You seem worried, I noticed, Shell,' she remarked, sounding genuinely concerned. 'What is it?'

He shrugged. 'Nothing worth mentioning, I guess.' He looked beyond her as he added, 'I'll be leaving tomorrow.'

'Must you go? You don't have to.'

'Yes, I do.'

She reached out and touched his hand. 'Oh, Shell, I am so sorry. I-I think I know how you feel about me now. But you must understand that there's only ever been one man for me, and that's Clint. But that doesn't mean you and I can't be the very best of friends, does it?'

'Reckon not.' Somehow he managed a smile. 'And I hope things work out the way you want, Amy. You deserve it.'

'Sweet Shell,' she said softly, and with a light, warm pressure on his arm, turned away and made for the house.

'Friends?' Dunbar murmured as he entered the stables. 'You'll always be more than that to me, Amy Blue-eyes . . . '

In the cool gloom of the stables he set to work at the work bench where he'd left Moe Archer's broken bridle harness. It needed patching before he could use it on the rig he would ride out on next day.

Searching for a punch on Rooney's tool bench his eye fell on Buckner's saddle resting on a tree. There was a bullet hole through the flap, testifying to how close things had been in that final battle at the canyon yesterday. Yet after a moment his attention was drawn away from the saddle to the saddle-bag. It was a make with which Dunbar was familiar. A Jordan Brothers courier's saddle always came equipped with a cleverly disguised enclosed false bottom for expensive or important items.

Naturally, he puzzled over what Buckner might be carrying that was so valuable. He even wondered idly if there might be something in there that would rid him of that oddly uncomfortable and suspicious feeling he'd had about Amy's lover right from the get-go.

He was actually reaching for the saddle before realizing what he was doing. With a soft curse he dropped his hand, collected the broken bridle harness and went outside to work on it.

'Just forget it, Dunbar,' he muttered to himself. 'He won, you lost, so take it like a man.'

★　★　★

It was late at night but lights still burned brightly in the canyon. The moon was silver and frogs croaked companionably around the spring following a brief flurry of rain. The desert could be a pleasant place at times like this, providing you didn't step on a rattlesnake.

Buckner and Amy returned from a stroll along the rim top. The couple had left hand-in-hand but there was considerable distance between them now as they approached the house. They weren't speaking and when Buckner sighted Dunbar's tall figure across by the corrals he left Amy without a word and headed directly across to him.

Shell was feeling mellow.

He'd shared a few drinks with Rooney while the couple was absent, and Stolbeck had gone so far as to concede that maybe he wasn't such a bad sort of young jasper after all. From Rooney Stolbeck that was rare praise indeed.

So he smiled amiably as Buckner came up. 'Clint,' he murmured. 'Enjoy your walk?'

There was no answering smile from Clint Buckner. 'Not specially,' he said. 'I'd like to talk to you, Dunbar.'

'Sounds serious.'

'It is.' As the man paused to light up a stogie Shell saw his face appeared tightly drawn and hard. Flicking the match away, Buckner began pacing to and fro before him. 'You mightn't like what I'm going to say, Dunbar,' he said in that same harsh tone, 'but you're going to listen.'

'Well, get it off your chest.'

'You're sweet on Amy, aren't you?'

Shell frowned. 'Are we back to that?'

'We sure are. You love her and you want her. Right?' Buckner nodded emphatically. 'Sure you do. So, maybe we can make a deal.'

Shell wondered if he'd heard right. 'A deal? What kind of deal?'

Buckner stood squarely before him, big and assured, eyes gimlet hard now. 'You have money, don't you, Dunbar? Sure, Amy told me. How much?'

'Well, maybe a thousand, but — '

'Enough. And that's just what it will cost. One thousand and Amy's yours.'

Shell stared incredulously. 'How's that again?'

'It's over and finished, me and her.' Buckner gestured at the house. 'It was all finished the day Rooney lost all his money, but I didn't get a chance to wind it up officially until now. No way was I ever going to marry into a poor family, my father would never allow it. I've got big things to do and places to go in this life, mister. I need money to get there but I don't need Amy. It's hard but true. So, do we have a deal?'

'I say you'd better get the hell away from me before I forget you saved my life yesterday, Buckner.'

A sneer rode the man's mouth. 'What? Did I tramp on your tender feelings? Well, maybe that's just because I know a hell of a lot more about life and how the world works than you do, bounty man. And I sure know everything has its price. Everything.' He sketched a derisive salute in the air as he turned away. 'Think it over.'

Shell stared down at his hands as the man strode off. They were shaking. He felt sick, angry and disgusted all at once, but quickly brought his emotions under control, thinking about Amy. His heart went out to her for she genuinely loved someone who was prepared to trade her for one thousand lousy dollars!

What the hell kind of man was that?

The question stuck in his mind,

gnawing at him, troubling him. He realized there was something about Buckner he'd been unaware of before, something underhanded maybe? While they were talking earlier the man had suddenly revealed a side of himself unseen before. He'd offered to sell Amy to him for a thousand bucks — for God's sake!

Suddenly he found himself thinking of that unusual saddle-bag which he'd been almost tempted to check out earlier. In light of what had just happened, that temptation was too strong to resist now. He needed to know anything he could find out about the man Amy loved.

He entered the stables quietly minutes later. He went directly to the saddle and felt for the hidden clip beneath the flap which he knew to be there. He opened the secret compartment in the special security section, rummaged in the contents to find assorted items — papers, spare shells, a set of diamond cufflinks.

The document was right at the bottom, tucked away beneath a concealing fold of leather. It was a stiff parchment of a kind he was well familiar with in his line of work.

Even before he opened it he had half-guessed what it might be.

★ ★ ★

The Stolbecks and Clint Buckner were sitting over coffee in the parlour a short time later when Dunbar walked in. He appeared pale and grim.

'Shell!' Amy cried sharply, rising. 'What is it?'

'I'm sorry, Amy,' he said, and really meant it. 'But this is something I have to do.' He turned and drew his .45 and angled it at Buckner. 'Hand over your gun, Clint.'

Buckner went white. 'Are you loco —?'

Dunbar reached out and plucked Buckner's six-gun from its holster.

'Shell!' Amy gasped, then broke off as Dunbar drew a folded sheet of stiff paper from his inside jacket pocket, which he flicked open. 'Will you tell them what this is, Buckner, or will I?'

Buckner had lost all colour, seemed unable to speak. Shell unfolded the document and spread it out beneath the lamplight. It was a Wanted dodger and its message was blocked out in solid black type on a yellow background. It read:

FOR MURDER AND
BANK ROBBERY!
WANTED

CLINTON BUCKNER OF
CASH COUNTY.
SIX FEET, STRONG BUILD,
BLACK HAIR AND BLUE EYES.
SON OF SENATOR
BARLOW BUCKNER.
$2,500 REWARD BEING OFFERED
BY THE COUNTY,
THE US MARSHAL'S OFFICE
AND THE WELLS FARGO
COMPANY!

It was Amy who broke the shocked silence first. 'Clint, what on earth does this mean?'

Yet Dunbar could tell instantly that this came as no surprise to her. She knew . . .

Buckner had lost all colour, yet his face was hard and dangerous. His eyes were cold as they flared at an impassive Dunbar.

'I knew you were crazy about Amy!' Buckner accused. 'That's what pushed you to go through a man's private — '

'Save the wounded victim act,' Dunbar said harshly. 'You're wanted and I'm taking you in.'

'No!' Amy cried. 'You don't understand, Shell. Clint told me about this. But he had nothing to do with that robbery and killing; he was framed by his father's political opponents. Isn't that so, Pa?'

'Dead right,' Rooney affirmed. 'You see, Dunbar, Amy and I always believed in Clint's innocence, and when I hit gold here I was able to help him out and hide him when the law was pressing him too close. But we're still fighting to get his name cleared and — '

'I reckon I read you only too plain, mister,' Dunbar cut him off. 'You had to know he was guilty, but you were so set on having Amy wed to a senator's son so the marriage would lift you back up to where you always wanted to be, that you'd do anything to keep him from being exposed. Go on, look me in the eye and tell me I'm wrong.'

Rooney Stolbeck seemed to disintegrate before their eyes as the accusation struck home. For what Dunbar said was so. Prestige ranked infinitely higher than justice in this man's world and he was shattered by the truth being revealed.

But Amy had the look of a vixen protecting her young as she faced Dunbar with blazing eyes.

'Clint is innocent!' she cried. 'It doesn't matter what that paper says, he didn't kill anyone! It's impossible. He's not a murderer!'

Dunbar nodded slowly. He could

almost understand her belief. Buckner didn't look, talk or act like a killer. And maybe if he hadn't seen the excitement in the man's face as he'd used a gun the night before, he might have almost believed her.

'We'll have to leave that for the judge, Amy,' he said tonelessly, clearly aware in that moment that he had fallen in love with this woman — who now must surely only hate him forever. He cleared his throat and added, 'This is my duty.'

The girl composed herself with an obvious act of will before replying now.

'Very well, Shell, you can have what you want.'

He frowned. 'I don't follow — '

'Me, Shell. You have just proven you want me so badly that you're prepared to frame the man I love. I sensed from the first you wanted me but I never imagined you'd go this far.' She raised her chin. 'Well, let him go and I'll marry you, do anything you want. Only don't let them hang him.'

It was the worst moment of Shell

Dunbar's life. 'You . . . love him that much?'

'More.'

Dunbar looked like a man who'd aged years in minutes. Yet when he spoke his voice was measured and controlled. 'I wish I could do what you ask, Amy. But if I let him go, I'd be betraying the people he's already killed and I'd be responsible for those he would certainly kill in the future. I couldn't live with that — '

He broke off as Buckner made his play. The sneak gun glittered in the light as it slipped from his sleeve where it had been released by Buckner's finger pressure on a spring. The tiny yet lethal weapon filled the man's hand and he was a split second away from pumping the lethal .22 slug into Dunbar's chest when Shell's fist exploded against his jaw and he crashed unconscious to the floor.

Shell would never forget the look in the eyes of the woman he loved as he said, 'I must . . . I must take him in.'

The trial, in San Paulo, of the People versus Clinton Buckner, drew a record crowd. It covered three days, but long before the jury retired the verdict was foreseen by one and all.

Clint Buckner was guilty as sin. The Wells Fargo attorneys produced a slew of witnesses who'd seen him cut down two payroll guards outside the bank and escape with the money. His father wept and revealed to the court that his only son had had a terrible violence inside him all his life and tried to explain it: 'Nobody put it there . . . it was something he was born with . . . a wildness, a devil within that made him lie and cheat . . . and finally kill.'

The jury unanimously found him guilty and the judge sentenced him to hang.

Ouside, Shell Dunbar shouldered his way roughly through the crowd to reach the Stolbeck buckboard. But father and daughter stared straight ahead and didn't speak as Rooney flicked the whip and got his mules moving.

They still didn't believe he'd had to do it.

They never would . . .

★　★　★

Ten miles north of San Paulo, the lone rider encountered an old mule wagon with the cut-under front gear. It was crammed with dark-haired Mexican children, and a careworn woman plied the reins.

'Señor!' she cried as he made to pass on by without a greeting. 'This is the way to San Paulo where the trial will be held?'

He reined in. 'You're on the right trail. But the trial is over.'

'Too late!' the woman sighed as the children gaped at him wide-eyed.

'You were going to the trial?' he frowned.

'Sí. You see, the man Buckner, he slew my husband and stole all we had

193

in Calaba in the spring. And this was after we had nursed him following a gunfight.' She spoke matter of factly, her eyes long emptied of feeling. 'I have come to see him die . . . unless he was set free?'

'No, he didn't go free . . . '

Dunbar sat in his saddle studying the family for a long minute in silence, aware that his grimness and bitterness seemed at last to be easing. For here was the proof that what he'd done had been right — and today for some reason he'd needed such affirmation. He had brought the law's just retribution to Clint Buckner for this woman's husband whom he'd slain; he had saved the next innocent man or woman who might have held out a helping hand to Buckner, the heedless butcher . . .

Abruptly he heeled his mount across to the mules, reached out to seize them by the head-harness, then turned the rig around. The woman began to protest but he held up a silencing hand.

'You don't really want them to see

any man hang,' he said roughly. 'That's for ghouls . . . not mothers and babies.'

His free hand unbuckled his money belt and he tossed it across her lap.

'Go back home and forget Clint Buckner the way I've got to, woman,' he said gruffly, and was out of sight by the time eager hands had clawed open the fat wads of reward money that packed it like Pandora's box.

THE END

THE VENGEANCE TRAIL

J. D. Kincaid

After saloon girl Kitty O'Hara shoots Billy Tranter in self-defence, she flees town and heads north out of Texas. Billy's brother, Texas Ranger Captain Johnnie Tranter, pursues Kitty — and he wants revenge for Billy's death. Johnnie's plans are thwarted, however, when Wolf Brennan's gang hold up Kitty's stagecoach and she escapes with the outlaws. Meanwhile, the famous Kentuckian gunfighter, Jack Stone, is on the case, and they don't come tougher or deadlier than Jack Stone.

LONG BLOWS THE NORTH WIND

Owen G. Irons

Brian McCulloch's only friend and partner is gunned down by Jason Grier and his prowling gang. They had set upon the pair, hoping to steal a cartload of valuable furs. Brian, wanting to avenge his friend and to prove himself a man, needs to track down Grier . . . but the trail is long and cold, and the storms he must pass through are more violent than he could have ever expected.

HELL IN THE MESQUITES

Daniel Rockfern

The name he gives is Green. Seemingly, just another drifting puncher. But you look again . . . and notice the whipcord frame — eyes that can change to icy menace in seconds. You'll see the matched Colts in the tied-down holsters, their butts smooth with use. Capable, and perhaps dangerous, you would be glad to have him on your side. He looks like a man who would know what to do in a tight spot and do it in a flash.

RENEGADE'S LEGACY

Rick Dalmas

The mystery man rode into town the day that they buried Big Al McCord. Some people suspected he was 'Dan McCord', a runaway kid returning after twenty years — and out for vengeance. His arrival shook the townsfolk, bringing turmoil and gunsmoke to the rangeland, panicking the corrupt officials and folk with a bad conscience. But Brett had his own agenda — and when they found out what it was, that part of Dakota would never be the same again.

A COFFIN FOR SANTA ROSA

Steve Hayes

Outlaw Gabriel Moonlight makes a promise to a dying friend. Ingrid Bjorkman wants him to bury her beside her late husband in Santa Rosa. However, she wants a Pinkerton to escort her coffin to Santa Rosa: the hanging rope awaits Gabriel in New Mexico. Forced by his love for her though, he takes on the whole sad task of her burial himself, accompanied by Ingrid's daughter, Raven. But Gabriel, living in the shadow of the rope, also faces betrayal . . .

THE HUNTING OF LOPE GAMBOA

Jack Sheriff

Texas Rangers Frank Carson and Eddie Brand have been unsuccessfully hunting outlaw Lope Gamboa for some time, but their luck seems to change when they ride into Yuma. A consignment of US gold is to be transported along the Oxbow Route by Conestoga wagon and the Rangers are convinced that Gamboa will attempt to steal the precious metal. As all factions close in on the lumbering Conestoga wagon, the trail leads inexorably to the Gila desert . . . and a bloody climax.